IN THE SPIRIT

NOVA BLAKE

IRIS BEAGLEHOLE

PROLOGUE: CONSTANCE

Constance Mōhio sat in her usual chair as dawn crept through the window, her bones creaking like the old villa around her, watching steam rise from her cup. The land around Kotahi Bay felt emptier now. Had done since word came of Sylvie's sudden passing.

"You always said you'd outlast me, old friend," Constance murmured, her fingers tracing the rim of the earthen cup, its glaze the deep blue-green of pāua shell. Strange, how quickly Sylvie had declined.

Constance frowned. Sylvie had given her this cup. Everything beautiful in this house seemed to carry her old friend's touch. Her white plaits, still thick despite her years, swung forward as she leaned to inhale the steam. Kawakawa tea, for memory and grief.

The herbs hung in great bundles from the ceiling beams – horopito, kawakawa, mānuka. So many years of gathering, of learning the old ways together. Above her head, tūī and pīwakawaka called their morning songs, but there was a note of warning in their voices today. They knew, as she did, that a great uncertainty spread out before them.

What did Sylvie's passing mean for Kotahi Bay...?

Constance touched the rich jade-green pounamu pendant at her throat, feeling the steady pulse of power there. The boundary still held, but for how long? The old guard were slipping away. Now she alone remained, and her own thread grew short.

Outside, the first rays of sun caught the tips of the pōhutukawa trees that lined her property, their red flowers in full bloom, always bringing festive cheer to the summer.

The younger ones would be here soon – Matai and Samantha – coming to discuss what must be done. But for now, in this quiet moment between night and day, Constance let herself feel the full weight of her grief. A mighty tōtara tree had fallen indeed.

As the sun rose higher, the sound of car tires on gravel drew her attention. Constance smiled despite her heavy heart. She levered herself up from the chair, joints protesting, and shuffled to put the kettle on again.

There was a friendly knock just before the back door creaked open – they knew better than to use the front, which was purely for show these days, its path overgrown with kawakawa forming a natural barrier, the magic subtle but effective at turning away those who didn't belong.

"Aunty!" Samantha's voice carried down the hallway, bright despite the early hour. Not blood relation, of course, but family all the same.

"In the kitchen, where else would I be?" Constance called back, setting out cups from the shelf.

Matai appeared first, ducking his head under the dried herbs. His tattoos shifted in the morning light, the protective runes flowing like water across his skin. He pressed a kiss to Constance's weathered cheek, setting a paper bag on the table.

"Fresh bread," he said. "And honey from my bees."

"Showing off again?" Constance raised an eyebrow at him. "Your bees make the best honey because you sweet-talk them."

"I prefer to think of it as diplomatic relations." He grinned, but it didn't quite reach his eyes.

They all felt Sylvie's absence, like a missing heartbeat in the rhythm of their small community.

Samantha drifted in, her blonde hair caught up in

a messy bun, wearing one of those flowing dresses that made her look more like a fairytale character than a serious witch. But Constance knew better – there was steel under all that gauze, and power in those silver-ringed fingers.

"I felt it," Samantha said, sinking into a chair. "When she...when Sylvie..." She swallowed hard. "The boundary rippled."

Constance nodded slowly, pouring tea for them all. "I felt it too. The pīwakawaka have been warning of it – listen to them now, how their song has changed."

They fell silent, hearing the urgent notes through the birds' morning chorus.

Matai's jaw tightened. "She wasn't supposed to go first," he said quietly. "She was the strongest."

"Strength isn't always enough." Constance settled into her chair with a sigh. "Sometimes, the mightiest trees fall first, making way for new growth." She stirred honey into her tea, watching the golden swirls. "Sylvie knew what was coming. She tried to prepare..."

"The granddaughter?" Samantha leaned forward. "Alyssa?"

"Mm." Constance's lips twisted. "That's a tangled root system if ever there was one. It's a concern, especially with the strange goings on at the council. Mrs Nolan cannot be trusted. She should be kept away from Alyssa. The girl has power – how could she not, with her bloodline? But she turned from it years ago. Sylvie spoke of her often, though mostly in regret."

"Something scared her away," Matai said. It wasn't a question.

"Yes." Constance watched a pīwakawaka dart to her windowsill, its tail fanning out as it landed, momentarily, before disappearing again. "Power without control, fear without understanding. A dangerous combination." The bird cocked its head, as if listening, then flew off with a sharp cry.

"But she's coming back now," Samantha pressed. "To claim the house, at least. That has to mean something."

"It means the wheels are in motion." Constance set her cup down with a decisive clink. "But claiming a house is one thing. Claiming a heritage – especially one you've rejected – that's another matter entirely. Especially when we don't know what really happened that night. No one understands Sylvie's power. She was always so cryptic about that."

"How can we help Alyssa then?" Samantha asked. "We don't know her, and we don't understand her magic – not properly."

"We'll do what we can," said Constance, firmly. "Give her some space and offer our support. That's all we can do. The rest will be up to her."

1

ALYSSA

Alyssa shut the front door and slid the bolt across, leaning against the weathered wood. She kept her limbs tucked inside the frame, out of sight from any prying eyes peering through the windows flanking the entryway. Her strawberry blonde hair was at an awkward length now, escaping the tidy bun she'd had it in, making her look more crazed than grieving. Her makeup was no doubt cracked and ruined, and the only decent dress she'd been able to locate was a touch too small.

As she stepped over the threshold, the air shifted – warmer than it should be given the drafty entryway, carrying an elusive scent reminding her of childhood visits: herbs and old wood, with an underlying current of something less definable.

Magic, though the thought of the word brought a constriction to her chest. The house seemed to exhale around her, settling, as if recognising her presence. Alyssa shoved the sensation away. It was just grief and exhaustion. Magic was not something she was allowed. Not ever.

All day she'd been drowning in a sea of other people's condolences and expectations. The constant noise, the awful small talk had been exhausting. Right now, the only thing she craved was blessed solitude and quiet. And to have this house – her house now – all to herself.

She inhaled deeply, held it, then exhaled and opened her eyes, taking in the foyer. It was one of those grand old villas she'd always fantasised about owning someday. If she was being completely honest, it was this specific house that had captured her imagination since childhood, though she'd never dared hope it would actually be hers. Dreams like that didn't come true for people like her.

Though once, she'd believed differently. Back when she'd spent summers here with Gran, learning about herbs and crystals, watching with wide-eyed wonder as her grandmother coaxed plants to grow and whispered to the earth. Before the incident... Before her mother had forbidden any mention of magic or Gran's "peculiarities." Before Alyssa had locked that part of herself away so thoroughly that she'd almost convinced herself it had never existed.

And of course, this house came at a terrible cost. Gran was gone, taken too soon. The only thing that made the intense grief easier to bear was that for some reason Gran had willed the house to Alyssa. The escape this gave her couldn't have come at a better time after everything that had happened – that fateful meeting with the doctor that preceded the break up with Grant...

Of course, Alyssa had long been suspicious there was something missing inside her, something wrong with her. But recent events had only driven that home.

Since then, she'd been drifting aimlessly, stuck in a thankless dead-end call-centre job, no clue what the future held. Unmoored by the news that she'd never be a mother.

She'd actually been planning to visit Gran for the first time in over a decade, desperate for the special brand of comfort and counsel Alyssa remembered from her childhood.

Alyssa felt like a failure in every possible way. Not only couldn't she give her ex the family he wanted, but she'd been a crappy granddaughter. She hadn't even known the old woman was ailing, despite their regular phone calls.

She should have known.

Alyssa gripped her stomach, sick with so much grief. Gran was the only one in the family who could have helped her pick up the pieces, but now she was gone and Alyssa had missed out on being here to comfort her or even to say goodbye.

"I wish you were still here," Alyssa sighed, an ache blooming in her chest. Raw grief battled with guilty relief and bittersweet nostalgia, tangling together until she couldn't tell how she truly felt. In time the emotions would settle, she told herself, for now she should just appreciate the house and try not to think about the future.

Buttons, Gran's aging cat, sauntered across the hardwood floor and twined himself around her ankles. Absently, Alyssa scooped him up, nuzzling her face into his soft fur as she gazed into the living room. She felt a slight chill. Buttons was colder than he had any right to be, but still comforting. Memories flooded back, overlaying the present. Dancing with Gran in circles on the worn carpet, reciting poetry by the crackling fire, learning to make little charms and spell pouches. All the magic they'd shared, now lost like autumn leaves scattered by a brisk wind.

“Of course, inheriting a house in a quirky town is the start of a thousand cosy mysteries,” she muttered to herself. And to top it all off, Gran was a witch. Everyone knew that. But what was Alyssa? She had the gift as Gran always said, but the magic itself...she couldn't think about it. Not after the incident.

Now that she was here, would her mother still talk to her? Or would she give Alyssa the silent treatment until she'd come to her senses and returned to her normal life?

She hadn't realised just how lonely inheriting Gran's house would feel; she knew no-one in this town, and the absence of friends and family made the silence that much more intense. The house seemed to whisper to her, secrets in the walls, magic thrumming under her feet. It recognised her, it knew her magic, even if she wanted to deny that part of herself.

A sudden sharp knock at the door startled her. Buttons yowled in protest as her arms tightened reflexively. "Sorry, sorry," she murmured, setting him down and smoothing her rumpled black dress. She finger-combed her messy hair, set her face into a suitable expression, and opened the door.

A reedy, uncomfortable-looking man stood on the step, tugging at his too-tight collar. "Miss Whenua? I'm Derek McDermott. The, uh, lawyer?" He said it like a question, as if not quite convinced of his own qualifications. And to be fair, he didn't look like a lawyer, or anyone she would trust with her last will and testament. They'd only spoken on the phone before now, and his appearance was utterly bland, which matched his voice.

Alyssa folded her arms. "Right. Hi...What can I do for you?" She kept her voice polite but brisk.

He glanced around, confirming the driveway was empty, then lowered his voice. "I know it's an imposition, but I must speak with you. Privately."

She frowned. "Look, I'm really not in the mood for—"

"Please, it's important. It won't take long." He held up a placating hand. "Your grandmother left something for your eyes only. I couldn't in good conscience give it to you in front of your...other relatives. They were rather..." He trailed off.

"Obnoxious? Pushy? Aggressive? Assh—"

"Just so," he said hastily, cutting her off. "Sylvie was beloved here, you see, so it was quite shocking how some of her family behaved."

"Believe me, I'm used to it," Alyssa said dryly. "I've dealt with their crap my whole life."

Derek hesitated, eyes darting around as if afraid of being overheard. "Sylvie hinted that there were things about this town, about your family history, that might put you in danger. I wasn't told the details, but she was adamant that you be careful. That you watch for signs."

Alyssa's fingers brushed against the worn wood of

the doorframe, and for a moment, she felt a spark – like static electricity but warmer, more alive. She jerked her hand away, but not before catching a glimpse of Derek's knowing look. He'd noticed something, though he was too polite – or too wary – to mention it.

"Signs of what?" Alyssa asked, a prickle of unease crawling up her spine.

"I don't know," he admitted. "She was rather cryptic. But she told me she believed you have the power to face whatever is coming. That it is your destiny."

Destiny. The word clanged through her like a discordant bell. Gran had always said Alyssa had a great fate ahead of her, but she'd stopped believing in fairy stories a long time ago.

Derek cleared his throat. "In any case..." He pulled out an old VHS tape and held it out to her. "Your grandmother was very insistent that this was for you alone."

"What is it?" Alyssa asked, staring at the outdated technology.

"I believe it's a personal message she recorded for you," he replied. "I haven't viewed the contents. She said it was private." He checked his watch, already edging back from the threshold. "Watch it when you're ready."

He thrust the case into her hands, then turned

and strode briskly back to his car before she could even thank him.

"Weird," Alyssa muttered as his taillights disappeared down the drive. "Very weird."

Strangest of all was imagining Gran, with her love of analogue antiques, recording a video message. The mental image conjured a wry smile before melancholy crashed back over her. She wasn't ready to see Gran's face again. Not so soon after watching her coffin lowered into the cold earth. But if Gran had taken the time to record something, it must be important.

As Alyssa contemplated the tape in her hand, another knock sounded at the door. She sighed, wondering if she'd ever get a moment's peace.

She opened the door to find a woman standing on the porch, her silver hair neatly coiffed, eyes twinkling behind wire-rimmed glasses. She wore a pale pink cardigan over a simple floral dress and carried a wicker basket, the aroma of freshly baked muffins wafting from beneath the checked cloth. Alyssa had a feeling she'd seen this woman at the funeral service, though that was all a blur.

"Alyssa, dear!" she exclaimed, her smile warm and grandmotherly. "I'm June Hardwick, a dear friend of Sylvie's. I thought you could use a proper welcome to the neighbourhood." She proffered the basket. "Blueberry muffins – Sylvie's favorite. Oh, the times we spent sharing these over a cup of tea!" June's gaze softened in remembrance.

Alyssa shook her head. Were blueberry muffins Gran's favorite? That didn't sound quite right, but it must be true because here was a sweet old woman telling her so. June's gaze swept the room, a fleeting look of calculation in her eyes before it was replaced by gentle concern. "My, you must be overwhelmed with all this. Why don't I help you sort through some of those boxes?" She pointed to a stack of boxes in the hall.

Alyssa hesitated, torn between her need for solitude and a desire not to piss off the neighbours before she'd had a chance to settle in. "That's very kind of you, June, but it's been a long day. I'm still trying to process everything. Maybe another time?"

June nodded, understanding in her eyes. "Of course, dear. You take all the time you need. I'm just two houses down on the right if you need anything." She set the basket on a nearby table. "Do enjoy the muffins. They always brought a smile to Sylvie's face."

As June left, Alyssa found herself alone once more, surrounded by the whispers of the old house, the lingering scent of fresh muffins, and the weight of the mysterious VHS in her hands.

She wandered through the house, trailing her

fingers along the papered walls. The patterns were faded and peeling in spots. She knew if she picked at them, she'd find old newspapers plastered underneath, a hidden archive of bygone years. To Alyssa, that was the allure of these old houses – the secrets buried within, waiting to be discovered.

Secrets all belonging to me now...A shiver rippled down her spine. Anticipation or trepidation? Both, if she was being honest.

As she made her way down the hallway, a floorboard creaked loudly under her foot, then a rumble sounded. Just a gust of wind rattling the windows, but Alyssa froze. All the windows were closed, and there was no sign of a draft. Another gust sent the gauzy curtains in the lounge billowing. A whisper seemed to curl through the room, snatches of indecipherable words. The hair on Alyssa's arms stood up. There was something strange about this house. She had the distinct feeling of being watched.

In the kitchen, she stopped and stared. It felt so familiar yet alien to her. She half-expected to see Gran puttering about, flicking on the kettle and pulling down two mugs for her famous hot cocoa. The best.

Alyssa set the VHS on the counter and went through the motions of making herself a cup of cocoa, trying to stave off the sense that Gran would appear and scold her for brooding.

Movement outside the window caught her eye. A white shape jutted out from the edge of the woods. As she watched, it turned and glided towards the house.

Alyssa's breath caught. The shape moved strangely, more floating than walking. Like something out of a horror movie.

And it was heading right for the door.

Heart pounding, Alyssa grabbed a knife from the block on the counter. She crept towards the back door, listening hard. Silence. Then, a thump on the porch, like something heavy being dropped.

She inched closer, knife raised. The door rattled in its frame as if shaken by an unseen hand. Alyssa's mouth went dry. The rattling stopped as abruptly as it began.

Holding her breath, she lunged forward and yanked the door open. The porch was empty. No sign of the figure in white.

But on the welcome mat sat a bouquet of dead flowers, as if someone had placed them there only moments before. Alyssa whirled around, scanning the yard. She caught a glimpse of white vanishing into the tree line. Was that long white hair, or a cloak?

"Hey!" she yelled. "Who's there?" But the figure was gone. It had moved far too quickly to be human, hadn't it?

Dread curled in Alyssa's stomach. Was Gran

trying to tell her something from beyond the grave? That lawyer had warned her to watch for signs that she was in danger. Was this what he meant?

With a shaking hand, Alyssa gathered up the dead flowers. They smelled sickly sweet, cloying. Like a funeral home. A thorn pricked her finger and she dropped them, watching a bead of blood well up.

She sucked the blood from her finger and glanced back into the shadowed house. The home that should have been a sanctuary now felt like a trap. What secrets had Gran kept from her?

2

ALYSSA

A bone-deep chill permeated the house, seeping under the thin blanket, waking Alyssa. She sat up, heart pounding, unnerved by the darkness that had fallen while she'd drifted off. Even the glow of the streetlights couldn't seem to penetrate the oppressive shadows that gathered in the corners of the room, clinging like cobwebs.

Shivering, she tossed aside the blanket and slipped her feet into Gran's worn slippers, the once-soft fabric now stiff with age. She drew the faded blue robe tighter around herself, imagining she could still catch the faint scent of her grandmother's lavender perfume clinging to the fibers. A quick glance at the antique clock on the bedside table told her it was 9:00 p.m., and her stomach rumbled insistently. The last thing she'd eaten was a few hasty bites of a club sandwich and a sausage roll at the post-funeral reception, the food sitting heavy in her stomach as she'd fielded the well-meaning but empty condolences from strangers.

She made her way down the stairs, flicking on lights as she went in a vain attempt to banish the gloom. Most of the heavy curtains were drawn against the night, but she knew that somewhere beyond the moth-eaten fabric, the last embers of the sunset were fading out over the horizon, like hopes burning down to ashes.

In that moment, a wave of loneliness crashed over her, so intense it stole her breath. She missed her flatmate Kelly fiercely, missed her brash laugh and easy companionship. On a balmy mid-December night like this, they should be out on the tiny porch of their shabby flat, cheap wine in hand, indie tunes filtering from ancient speakers as the BBQ cooled down from dinner, the air perfumed with jasmine from the tangle of vines on the neighbouring fence.

Alyssa made her way to the old-fashioned kitchen, the black and white tiles icy through the thin soles of her slippers.

The house creaked around her, but not with its usual welcoming warmth. Fine cracks spiderwebbed across the kitchen window frame, spreading like frost.

Something was wrong. The house's protective magic was failing, and Alyssa had no idea how to fix it.

She swung open the retro fridge, faded yellow paint peeling around the edges, and stared at the meagre offerings. A few condiments, a stick of butter, the heels of a loaf of bread that Gran used to always keep in the fridge so it wouldn't go mouldy before she could finish it. Alyssa's vision blurred as she remembered all the times Gran would rescue the stale ends to feed the ducks down at the creek, Alyssa dancing alongside her, both of them laughing as the birds squabbled over the scraps.

She pulled out the butter and bread, slathering the slightly dry slices with generous pats of butter and Gran's homemade blackberry preserves, the purple-black jam staining her fingers like ink. Like blood.

As if sensing her distress, Buttons appeared, squeezing through the cat flap and winding around her ankles, purring like a rusty engine. Alyssa scooped him up, pressing her face into his cool fur as she carried him to sit at the small kitchen table. "Oh, Buttons," she murmured. "I miss her so much already. What are we going to do, hmm?"

Buttons blinked slowly at her, then head-butted her chin gently before settling into a loaf on her lap, purring so loudly that she wasn't sure how he managed not to vibrate with it. Despite everything,

Alyssa felt her lips curve into a small smile. At least she wasn't entirely alone.

A memory surfaced: herself at seven, cross-legged in Gran's garden, giggling as tiny purple flowers bloomed between her palms.

"Magic flows like water, love," Gran had said, her eyes twinkling. "You don't force it. You guide it." Such simple magic then, pure and joyful. Before fear had crept in. Before the fire.

Her gaze fell on the innocuous VHS case sitting on the worn Formica tabletop, a coaster still stuck to the bottom from some long ago cup of tea. Gran had never been one for technology. There was no note, nothing to hint at what might be on it, so she got up and trudged through to the lounge, shoving the rest of the bread into her mouth as she crouched to insert the disc.

Once she settled on the couch, Buttons firmly ensconced on her lap, she pressed play and waited. The screen was black for a minute, and then Gran appeared, sitting on the very same couch as Alyssa, in almost exactly the same position.

"By now, everything is done. I'm buried and hopefully you're sitting on the couch at your new house." Gran sighed. "I wish I'd been able to see you before I passed, but I know how hard it was...after everything. I should have been more careful..."

Gran glanced away from the camera and then back again. "I know this is the last thing you want to think about, my darling. You used to understand before...well. You know. But you must remember that it wasn't all bad. The magic...you must remember how fun it was! All those times we used to dance...? And the little bundles of herbs we used to make? I never really explained all of that, not properly. Never got the chance. Your mother got scared, and stopped letting you visit before we could really get to the heart of it. I should just come right out and say it, shouldn't I? You're going to find out sooner rather than later."

Alyssa flinched. She didn't want to hear it. She wanted to switch off the screen or better yet, push the TV set over and smash it so that she never had to go any further, but, like watching a train wreck, she couldn't look away.

"We're witches, dear one," Gran's recorded voice said. "It runs thick in our blood, you and me especially. Your mother has it in her, though she never wanted anything to do with it. She thought it made her a freak, and in a way it does, but that's nothing to be ashamed of. She turned her back on magic and she couldn't bear the thought of you getting involved, either. I had promised not to teach you, but I couldn't help myself. You're so strong, and being here in Kotahi Bay makes the connection that much stronger. I just wanted to pass on our family legacy. I hope that some of it stuck, because you're going to need those skills."

Gran took a sip of water, fingers shaking, and pursed her lips.

Alyssa felt goosepimples prickle her skin. She had known about the magic. Had made the same choice as her mother, and yet there was part of her that missed it, felt the loss acutely, like she'd cut off a limb.

"There is no easy way to tell you this, but the reason I gave the house to you is because we need you. The whole bay...we need your magic to help maintain the barrier, to keep this place safe. I know that's a lot to take in. But that's not all."

Gran took a deep breath. She looked pale and drawn, worry clearly eating away at her. "Our family power has been bolstered by a powerful spirit for generations. Now, this is very important, so listen closely."

Gran leaned forward, and Alyssa found herself doing the same.

"For over a century, the women of our family have kept an evil spirit confined in a box, bound safely inside the house. It was my duty, and now it is yours. There are spells in my grimoire – the one with the red cover is what you'll need first. I don't know how many days I've been gone from the house, but it's important that you go now. Get the book, follow the spell to the letter, and rebuild the protections placed on the house. We can't let him escape. Go, do it now, as quickly as you can."

The screen went black, though the counter kept ticking like there was more to come. Alyssa stayed glued to the couch, her fingers digging into the worn fabric. Nothing else flashed up on screen, so after a moment she turned it off and sat in silence.

Seeing Gran on that recording, sitting in the same spot on the same faded floral couch, had been a punch to the gut, ripping open the barely-scabbed wound of Alyssa's grief.

She glanced towards the dark hallway that led to the stairs. Should she try to find the book, or skip forward on the VHS to see if there were any more instructions from beyond the grave. But the thought of delving further into this unknown world of magic and spirits Gran had dumped on her shoulders...it was too much. Not now, when she could barely hold herself together. Maybe this was all some weird dream, and tomorrow everything would make more sense.

What harm would one more night do?

But could she leave it until the morning if Gran was telling the truth? Alyssa didn't want to think about witchcraft or things that went bump in the night. Every time she did, flashes of the past returned to haunt her. Alyssa feared that was exactly what Gran's message was about, and this was just one more attempt to get her to reclaim her power.

Sighing, Alyssa gently displaced Buttons and headed upstairs to Gran's room. If she was going to take on this insane responsibility, she needed all the information she could get. She dropped to her knees by the bed and pulled out the box of books, flipping through aged pages filled with Gran's spidery handwriting, searching for any further clues or guidance.

As she turned the brittle pages, a folded sheet of paper slipped out from between two leaves and fluttered to the floor.

Something inside her rang like an alarm bell.

This is important...

Heart pounding, Alyssa snatched it up, unfolding it to reveal what looked like a crude map of the house sketched in faded ink. But something seemed off. It took a moment for Alyssa to realise what it was, but as she traced the lines with her index finger, there, in the basement, was a room she'd never seen before.

Alyssa frowned. She'd explored every inch of this house as a child, and she'd certainly never come across any secret rooms. But then again, it seemed there was quite a lot her Gran had kept hidden from her.

Propelled by curiosity, Alyssa grabbed a flashlight

from the bedside drawer and ventured down the narrow wooden steps to the chilly basement. She'd always found it creepy down here as a kid, the dank musky cement walls and cobwebbed corners fuelling her imagination with thoughts of prisoners left to rot in hidden oubliettes and vengeful ghosts lurking just out of sight. The faded map trembled in her hand as she swept the weak beam of the torch over the junk-filled space – boxes of mothball-scented furs, a broken sewing dummy standing sentinel in the corner, its blank face leering at her from the shadows.

The basement had always emanated a strange energy, even when she was a child. Back then, she'd attributed it to an overactive imagination, but now... The air grew thicker with each step down, heavy with accumulated magic. Old spells layered like sediment, marking generations of witchcraft. Her skin prickled with recognition, muscle memory stirring despite years of determined forgetfulness.

Modern houses sometimes had basements that were all concrete and utility. But this...The walls here were stone, worn smooth by time and touch, seeping a dampness that felt more like energy than water.

Nothing she hadn't seen before...until a flicker of movement in the torch beam made her heart leap into her throat. A rat? She waved the light wildly, catching a glint on the far wall, just behind a mouldy stack of

National Geographics. Easing closer, Alyssa reached out with a shaking hand and tugged on the magazines. The whole stack tumbled to the side...revealing the clear outline of a door set flush into the wall, the rusting handle reflecting the light.

"No way..." Alyssa breathed. She checked the map again, ice trickling down her spine as she confirmed she was in the right spot. She grabbed the handle and tugged. It resisted at first, so she propped the torch on the fallen stack of magazines and gripped the handle with both hands. The hinges squealed in protest, but with a hard tug it flew open, releasing a gust of stale, cold air that smelled like secrets and time.

Snatching up the torch, Alyssa stepped cautiously over the threshold into a small, low-ceilinged room. Her skin tingled as she moved into the room and a new sensation settled in her gut. It was like...coming home. Except that she'd never set foot in this room in her life.

It was bare except for a large wooden chest in the centre, its surface covered in strange symbols that seemed to shift and dance in the darkness. An old-fashioned hurricane lamp sat atop a rough wooden table shoved against the wall, along with a lighter, and with trembling fingers Alyssa managed to light it, casting a soft golden glow over the eerie space.

Alyssa's fingers traced the strange symbols carved

into the chest's surface. Each one sent a jolt through her system, like touching a live wire. But instead of electricity, it was...something else. Something that made the air taste like ozone and summer storms. "Stop it," she muttered, jerking her hand back. But she couldn't stop her mind from translating the symbols, knowledge bubbling up from some deep place she'd tried to keep buried: Protection. Binding. Containment. She'd learned this, once. Sitting cross-legged on Gran's worn rug while the old woman traced the shapes in salt, explaining how each line and curve channelled power. How magic wasn't just about intention, but about understanding the ancient language of symbols that connected witch to earth to sky. A memory surfaced – Gran teaching her to draw a simple protection ward. "Magic flows like water, love. You don't force it. You guide it. Channel it. Like this..." The chalk had felt so natural in her hand then. Everything had felt natural before the fire. Before Miri's screams. Alyssa's throat tightened. She could still smell the smoke, still feel the magic surging out of control. She'd sworn then – never again. Magic was too dangerous in her hands. But now, looking at these symbols, she felt that old pull. That sense of rightness, of connection to something vast and ancient. Her fingers itched to trace the patterns, to feel that spark of recognition.

The room thrummed with contained power, pressing against her skin, her mind. Symbols carved into the stone walls caught the light oddly, seeming to shift when she wasn't looking directly at them. They reminded her of the marks Gran used to draw in salt on windowsills during storms, though she'd never learned their meaning. Now they sparked something in her memory – a language she'd once begun to learn before everything went wrong.

Her fingers traced one symbol unconsciously. A jolt of energy shot up her arm, and for a split second, she saw a flash of memory: Gran teaching her about protective wards, showing her how to channel power through simple shapes. Younger Alyssa had absorbed it all eagerly, delighting in each new magical discovery. Before the fire...

Alyssa jerked her hand back, forcing the memories away. But she couldn't shake the feeling that the room recognised her, had been waiting for her.

She ran her fingers over the walls, which seemed to have been hewn from stone. Patches of moss clung to them, creating a lush setting. It felt like if she turned off the lamp she might discover glowworms clinging to the ceiling.

"What on earth were you hiding down here, Gran?" she whispered, the sound swallowed by the room's deep, waiting silence. Goosebumps raced over her skin as she moved to kneel before the chest, brushing away the thin film of cobwebs to reveal a heavy iron padlock. But the key was already there, hanging from a bit of twine, as if Gran had known Alyssa would find her way to this moment.

The lock opened with a heavy clunk, the lid lifting with a groan of un-oiled hinges to reveal a trove of books, loose pages, jars filled with strange powders and what looked horribly like bones. Hopefully not human.

But it was the leather-bound journal resting atop the arcane miscellany that arrested Alyssa's attention, the looping of Gran's initials embossed on the red cover in flaking gold leaf.

Hands shaking harder now, Alyssa lifted out the journal, a small key tumbling from the pages to land in her lap. She picked it up, admiring the intricate pattern adorning the key's surface, before setting it aside and opening the journal to the first age-spotted page. The date in the corner was from over a hundred years ago, written in old loopy handwriting and that was not Gran's. It was clear that an assortment of older entries had been rebound into this grimoire.

As she turned the pages, phrases seemed to leap out at her, words that sent chills chasing themselves up and down her spine. "Binding spell", "blood magic", "shades of necromancy". And everywhere, repeated like a drumbeat, a warning: "The revenant must not be freed. The consequences would be catastrophic."

Alyssa swallowed hard, the musty air suddenly choking. Gran had been deadly serious. This was no idle threat. The danger was real, and it was now Alyssa's duty to keep it contained...apparently she had no choice.

We'll see about that! The rebellious inner voice rose up – the part of her, long dormant, the traits that her ex-boyfriend had done his best to suppress, were now in full swing and no one was going to tell her what to do. Not even from beyond the grave. A burst of rage that Gran had decided to leave this all in her lap threatened to come out on a scream. Instead, she snapped the journal closed, the sound unnaturally loud in the pressing silence. She needed time to process this, to read Gran's words in depth and to determine what she wanted to do.

Her eyes fell on the small gleaming key she'd set aside, and on a hunch she pulled the contents of the chest out and scrabbled around the edges of the bottom.

There. She'd known it would be there. Alyssa lifted the false bottom of the chest to reveal a small, intricately carved wooden box, with a hole just the right size for the key. Her fingers trembled as she held the box and inserted the key, as if it threatened to leap out of her hand given the chance.

The lock clicked open easily and she held her breath as she opened the lid, half expecting a vengeful spirit to woosh out at her.

All it released though was a dusty puff of air, a faint trace of old cedar and snow. Inside was lined with a coarse woven fabric, nestling a necklace. Alyssa reached in, fingers hovering over the item before she steeled herself and lifted out a necklace with five glass beads that looked like they held a universe each. It was strung on a fine chain and glimmered in the lamp light. The piece was warm to the touch and seemed to vibrate with a strange energy; not necessarily malevolent, but not welcoming either. Almost as if it was waiting for her to imbue it with her own emotion. A runic symbol was etched into the surface of the largest glass bead, one that tugged at her memory. She'd seen it before, in the margins of Gran's hidden books, scrawled on scraps of paper that the old woman would hastily tuck away when a young Alyssa entered the room.

Without thinking about it, she lifted the necklace and clasped it around her neck, slipping the chain beneath her shirt. The beads felt warm against her chest, made a tingle of magic wash over her skin, down her body and back up again, as if it were scanning her for something.

Alyssa's head swam, her breath coming short. Her skin tingled and her senses felt overwhelmed; this was too much, too strange. The walls of this hidden room were pressing against her. She needed air, needed space to think. She gathered up the box, and the grimoire, and fled the confines of the hidden room, letting the door swing shut behind her with a thud like a coffin closing.

She stumbled up the steps to the kitchen, Buttons twining around her ankles and meowing plaintively, as if sensing her distress. She dumped her discoveries onto the table and locked the door to the basement, as though she could shut away everything she had just learned with that action. Her hands went to her neck, poised to remove the necklace, but then they fell away along with the idea.

With shaking hands, she put the kettle on and sank down at the table, staring sightlessly at the pile of secrets she'd unearthed. When the kettle began to whistle, she started violently, knocking over her mug and sending a splash of cold tea across the worn wood.

As she mopped it up with a dishtowel, Alyssa caught a flicker of movement out of the corner of her eye. She whipped around, heart in her throat, but there was nothing there. Just the old lace curtains stirring in a breath of wind from the cracked window. But she could have sworn she'd seen a pale figure reflected in the glass, hovering just over her shoulder.

Alyssa shook her head, trying to dislodge the crawling sense of unease. She was just tired, and spooked from all these revelations. Waiting to see a ghost in every corner of every room. She didn't even believe in ghosts! At least, she hadn't. She needed sleep, needed to approach this with a clear head in the morning light. It was all too much right now.

She tucked Gran's grimoire under her arm and trudged upstairs, Buttons close at her heels. But as she passed the darkened living room, she couldn't shake the prickling feeling of eyes on her back, boring into her from the shadows.

The grimoire seemed to pulse against her side, like a warning.

Alyssa shuddered and hurried to her room, locking the door firmly behind her.

But as she lay in the gathering dark, listening to Buttons' soft snores from the end of the bed, Alyssa couldn't suppress the small, treacherous voice whispering in the back of her mind that maybe, just maybe, she wasn't cut out for this. That when it came down to it, she'd be nothing but a pale spectre herself.

3

THE GHOST

He stretched against the binds digging into his spirit like chains of iron. And then something popped. Snapped. One of the links had been loosened and he could *breathe*.

The house smelled good. Full of latent magic, powerful and earthy.

It tasted like *them*. The ones who had bound him, locked him away.

But someone had made a mistake. Had let things slide.

Freedom. It was all he wanted. Freedom and perhaps revenge for the wrongs done to him. Someone was going to pay.

4

ALYSSA

Alyssa could hear birds chirping outside and sunlight glinted through the curtain and off the mirror, right into her eyes. She pulled the pillow over her head and tried to shut out the noise on the street. Despite this being a small town, there were still cars, and kids chatting as they walked past, the ring of a bike bell chimed.

She wanted to stay in the warmth of the blankets, but she was fully awake now and the need to pee had come over her, as did the itch to have a long hot shower and wash away all the disturbing thoughts of the night before.

Morning routine complete, she made her way to the kitchen and flicked the kettle on. She made her coffee the easy way, scoffing at how Kelly would have scolded her. Kelly always had to do things 'the right way'. Alyssa rolled her eyes, though the ache in her chest reminded her how much she missed her best friend.

Maybe Alyssa could convince her to come down for a few days...

She glared at the dishes in the sink as she slathered another piece of bread with blackberry jam, half hoping that Gran would come back as a ghost and keep her company. If there had to be a ghost in the house, why couldn't it be her?

Alyssa sighed. Gran wasn't coming back; if she were going to, she'd have been wailing and moaning at Alyssa for not tidying up after herself the night before.

As she ate, Alyssa's thoughts kept drifting back to the hidden room in the basement. The strange symbols etched into the chest, the jars of mysterious powders and what looked like bones, the old book, filled with cryptic references to scary-sounding magic. What exactly had Gran been involved in? It felt far more serious than the small magics they had done together when Alyssa was a kid.

She shuddered, a chill racing down her spine despite the warm sunlight streaming through the window. Last night's discoveries had shaken her deeply, dredging up old memories she'd tried hard to bury. The acrid smell of smoke, Miri's screams, the angry red burns marring her friend's skin...

She squeezed her eyes shut, forcing the images away. She couldn't let the past control her, not when Gran had trusted her enough to leave her this...legacy. If – and it was a big if as far as she was concerned – dark forces were at work, she had to find a way to stop them. Even if it meant embracing the power she'd rejected for so long.

The phone rang, its jingle echoing through the kitchen so loudly that Alyssa spilled coffee on her hand. "Crap!" She put the cup down and reached for the receiver, holding it between her shoulder and head. "Hello?"

"Am I speaking to Miss Whenua?"

"Ah, yeah, who is this?" She licked the coffee off her hand and took another bite of the bread. It felt strange that anyone would be calling for her, but then by now everyone in the town would know that Sylvie's granddaughter was in town.

"It's Mrs Leticia Nolan, from the preservation society."

"Okay..." Preservation society? What fresh hell was this? "Err...What can I help you with?"

"I understand that you've taken possession of Sylvie's house, and I wanted to know when I could come over and discuss a few things with you."

"What about?” Alyssa asked abruptly, before deciding to be more polite. After all, she lived in this town. For now, anyway. It wouldn’t hurt to play nice. “Sorry, I'm still getting my head around owning the place and I don't really know why you need to speak to me. I'm not planning on making any changes to the house at this point, anyway."

"It's about the ghost," Mrs Nolan said, quite frankly.

Alyssa let out a sigh. So much for this ghost being a secret. Or fictional. "Okay. Right. Well, how about two?"

"Two would be wonderful. Thank you, Miss Whenua."

"Call me Alyssa, please."

"Certainly," Mrs. Nolan agreed. A hopeful tone entered the woman’s voice. "You don't think there's any chance you could whip up a batch of your grandmother's scones?"

"Scones? What..." Alyssa frowned.

“Oh yes,” Mrs Nolan continued. “Sylvie was famous for her scones around here. We’ll all miss them dearly, and her of course. We’re hoping you can keep up the family legacy.”

Alyssa sighed again, feeling the tendrils of the woman’s expectations seeping down the phone line. "I don’t know about scones, but I'll see what I can do."

"Wonderful. I'll see you at two."

Alyssa hung up the phone and glanced around the kitchen. She didn't feel like her bread now, but she sculled back her now lukewarm coffee and appraised the situation.

She was now in possession of a house, with a ghost, and apparently the entire town thought that she would just slip right into her grandmother's role; and make the perfect scone. She had a feeling they were all going to be mighty disappointed. And suddenly, she wasn't sure she really wanted this kind of life after all. In fact, she wanted nothing more than to get out of here.

Alyssa grabbed her bag from the hall, checking that her car keys were there before locking the house behind her. Or maybe she should have just left it open so the ghost could get out and everyone else could take what they wanted – to hell with this legacy!

Alyssa made it to the footpath before the mournful meow of Buttons drew her attention back to the house. He sprang from the bushes, far too spryly for someone his age, and brushed up against her leg, sending a shiver over her skin, demanding in that feline way that she reach down and scratch his chin, before he attempted to lead her back inside.

As Alyssa gazed down at the cat, a sudden realisation struck her like a bolt of lightning. Buttons had been Gran's cat for as long as she could remember. But cats didn't live that long...did they? An icy prickle crawled up her spine.

She watched him walk, tail swishing in the air. Her gaze moved up to take in the house. Had she even stopped to look at it from outside yet? To remember what it felt like to come here every summer? She had loved being here, the sense of freedom from the mundane world, the thrill of possibility that being with her grandmother had held; she never knew what the old woman might unveil to her. Delicious secrets just between the two of them.

Gran had left her this place for a reason, like she was the only one in the family who could continue the legacy – even though it wasn't one Alyssa had asked for. Sometimes, though, people got what they needed, not what they wanted.

And what did she even want? She had been floating for so long, keeping busy so that she didn't have to address the lack in her life.

To admit that she secretly dreamed of running a shop, designing jewellery and maybe even clothing – quirky stuff. Kind of like the knickknacks and crafts she'd made with Gran when she was younger.

Witch things, Alyssa realised with a start. *Witch things. Damn it all.* She did have it in her blood, had a yearning for it before even properly understanding what 'it' was.

She left the cat sitting on the welcome mat and headed to the store, grabbing fresh milk, cream, more bread, and some other essentials before heading back to the house. It loomed before her, sunlight striking the front windows and making it seem brighter than it had a right to.

As she approached the porch, a flicker of movement in one of the windows caught her eye.

Alyssa gasped.

A pale figure hovered just beyond the glass, gone between one blink and the next.

Was it the same ghostly shape she'd seen last night, the same one leaving dead flowers on the doorstep?

The house suddenly felt more menacing than welcoming, full of dark secrets waiting to ensnare her.

She opened the side gate, escaping out to the garden.

A pīwakawaka flitted around her as she walked the overgrown path, its tail fanning like a tiny compass. Gran used to say these fantail birds were messengers, sometimes harbingers of change. Now one seemed to be guiding her back towards the house, as if it had a message.

Alyssa sighed. "You're right," she said to the bird. "I can't run from this."

There was unfinished business here. Business that it was up to her to deal with. But she couldn't live in Gran's house as it was, like some sort of mausoleum. Of course, Alyssa had nowhere else to go, but that didn't mean she had to lie down and surrender to Gran's legacy. No. She was going to make it *her* house, not a shrine to her dead grandmother. No matter how much she loved Gran, Alyssa wasn't just going to slip into the role others were assigning her; she was only just beginning to figure out who she was on her own again. She could accept that witchiness ran in her veins, but she wasn't sure about this whole ghost business.

And there was no way in hell she was making scones. Instead, she made up a batch of small pancakes, and laid out the muffins June had dropped off the day before. They were still fresh enough, though she hadn't been able to bring herself to eat one yet. Something strange about the smell of them.

Alyssa busied herself with tidying the house, sorting through Gran's eclectic collection of antiques and oddities. She lingered over a display of intricate blown glass witch balls, remembering how Gran had taught her they could ward off evil spirits. If only it were that simple. Alyssa felt a sudden chill and reached for the necklace that rested against her chest. Beneath it, her heart was pounding.

A knock at the door made her jump.

Alyssa smoothed down her blue dress and ran a hand through her tousled hair as a sharp knock sounded again. She'd been dreading this meeting with Mrs Nolan, but she pasted on a smile as she pulled open the door, determined to at least pretend she had everything under control.

The older woman stood on the stoop, thin lips pursed disapprovingly as she took in Alyssa's dishevelled appearance. She wore a severe charcoal suit that looked like it had been tailored for someone a few sizes smaller, the buttons straining over her ample bosom.

"Miss Whenua," she said crisply. "May I come in? I don't wish to take up too much of your time." Her tone implied she highly doubted Alyssa had anything better to do.

"Of course," Alyssa replied, saccharine sweet. "Please, join me in the kitchen. Can I offer you some tea or coffee?"

Mrs Nolan sniffed as she stepped over the threshold. "Just water, thank you."

She followed Alyssa down the narrow hallway, sensible heels clicking on the aged hardwood. Alyssa could feel the weight of her gaze on the back of her neck, silently judging the peeling wallpaper and dusty wainscoting. She wanted to tell the woman to take her shoes off, but at that moment it felt like Mrs Nolan had more of a claim to be here than she did.

In the kitchen, Mrs Nolan lowered herself primly into a chair at the scrubbed wooden table. Her brow furrowed as she took in the plate of small pancakes Alyssa had hastily assembled, tops glistening with jam and cream, along with the muffins June had brought over. Clearly, they hadn't been what she was expecting.

“I'm afraid I didn't have time to make scones," Alyssa said, forcing her face not to betray the petty delight she felt at disappointing the older woman.

Mrs Nolan sniffed. "Pity. Your grandmother's scones were legendary." Her sharp eyes roved over the kitchen, as if marking every way in which Alyssa had already made her mark, no matter how small. "I see you've been...exploring."

Alyssa bit back a smirk as she grabbed a pikelet and popped it whole into her mouth before taking the seat across from her guest. She might as well cut straight to the point of this visit. She reached for a muffin, but Mrs Nolan snatched it from her hand, and then grabbed the plate the rest sat on, moving promptly to dump them in the bin.

“What the hell?” Alyssa exclaimed, not sure

whether to be more surprised by the speed that Mrs Nolan moved, or her actions.

“They’ve gone bad.” Mrs Nolan’s nostrils flared. “How you couldn’t tell that is beyond me. From June, I gather? I wouldn’t trust her cooking if I were you.”

Alyssa let out a breath and tried to relax her body. Surely June hadn’t given her bad muffins, and they certainly hadn’t had long enough to get stale. More than ever, she just wanted to get this woman out of the house. "So," she said. "A ghost. What's that got to do with the historical society?"

Mrs Nolan folded her hands on the table, fixing Alyssa with a potent stare. "Miss Whenua, I'm not sure you grasp the full import of your position here. Kotahi Bay is...special. We respect the old ways. The hidden mysteries." She leaned forward, voice dropping. "Your grandmother was an integral part of that. A pillar of the community. And now, that mantle falls to you."

Alyssa nearly choked on her pikelet. She swallowed hard, fighting the urge to cough. "I'm sorry, what? Are you saying the town expects me to, what, take up witchcraft? Perform rituals and spells to keep the boogeyman locked in the basement?"

Mrs. Nolan's nostrils flared, two bright spots of color appearing on her cheeks. "Your grandmother took her responsibilities as one of the guardians of this town very seriously. I had hoped you would show the same respect for her legacy."

"No offense," Alyssa said, pushing to her feet, "but I don't see how my 'responsibilities' are any of the historical society's business. Far as I can tell, if there is a ghost in my house, it's my problem to deal with. No one else."

Mrs Nolan rose as well, drawing herself up to her full height. It wasn't very impressive. "Miss Whenua, you may not like it, but as the new mistress of this house, you have a duty to this town. One that has been passed down your family line for generations. I suggest you think very carefully before shirking it."

"Yes, well, it's quite an adjustment," Alyssa said, trying to direct the conversation to safer ground. "I'm still sorting through everything."

"Of course, of course." Mrs Nolan's eyes snapped back to Alyssa's face. "And the ghost? Any sightings?"

Alyssa hesitated. She didn't want to reveal too much, not when she still had so many unanswered questions herself. "Nothing concrete," she hedged. "Just...a creepy feeling."

Mrs Nolan leaned forward, a glint in her eye that was almost hungry. "Feelings can be very powerful things, Miss Whenua. Especially in a house like this. With a history..."

"What do you mean?" Alyssa asked warily. A bead

of sweat trickled down her spine despite the morning chill.

"Let's just say your grandmother was involved in more than just scones and doilies." Mrs Nolan's smile was sharp as a blade. "She had...gifts. Gifts that seem to run in the family."

"I'm sure I don't know what you mean," Alyssa said coolly, spine stiffening. "Now, if there's nothing else..."

"Oh, there's plenty else." Mrs Nolan's voice dropped low and she stepped closer. "Aren't you curious to learn more about your powers?"

Alyssa's temples pounded. Part of her desperately wanted to know more. But a larger part, the part that still woke up screaming from nightmares of fire and pain, quailed at the thought.

"I think you should go," she said firmly, gesturing towards the front door.

Mrs. Nolan looked like she wanted to argue, but something in Alyssa's face must have convinced her. She gathered her purse, pausing on the kitchen threshold to look back.

"You can't run from your destiny forever, Miss Whenua," she warned, gimlet eyes glinting. "Sooner or later, you'll have to embrace what you are. What you're meant to be. And when you do...I'll be waiting."

With that, she spun on her sensible heel and marched out of the kitchen. A moment later, the front door slammed with enough force to rattle the windows.

Alyssa let out the breath she'd been holding and walked slower down the hallway, flicking the lock on the front door before she returned to the living room. Her gaze strayed back to the wooden box on the coffee table.

Slowly, half against her own volition, Alyssa crossed the room and reached out to touch it. The instant her fingers brushed the carved symbols, a jolt ran up her arm.

Alyssa stared at it, mesmerised.

"No," she said firmly, placing it back on the table as carefully as if it were a grenade. "Not today."

5

ALYSSA

Alyssa had just slumped onto the couch when there was another knock at the door. No doubt Mrs Nolan returning because she'd forgotten to deliver one of her points. She shoved to her feet and stomped towards the door, swinging it open.

"What now?" she said, wincing as she saw that it was actually June standing on the doorstep, holding a thermos in one hand, the other still raised as if she was about to knock again.

"Are you quite alright, dear?" June asked, raising a superbly crafted eyebrow. Alyssa might have to ask the woman where she got her brows done because right now hers were more like caterpillars than refined body hair.

Letting out a sigh, Alyssa let the tension drain from her body as she leaned against the door frame. "Sorry. I thought you were Mrs Nolan, back for another round of haranguing."

"That woman," June said. She pressed her lips into a fine line, as though taking the age old wisdom of not saying anything at all, if you couldn't say something nice. Alyssa should probably follow that too.

"She was quite insistent I continue in Gran's footsteps." Alyssa shook her head. "Why me?" She knew she sounded childish; most people would be thrilled to have a house, a place in the world, all delivered to them on a condolence card for the loss she'd suffered. And she was grateful, for the house, for Gran. Even for the memories of the past that were returning with each day that she stayed there.

June gave her an assessing look, top to bottom, as if sizing her up. It had been days since the funeral, but Alyssa was sure she looked less put together than ever before. She'd been so intent on getting the house cleaned out, on picking through the past – and ignoring the spectre looming over everything – that she hadn't stopped to consider her appearance or the way that the people of this town might view her.

"It doesn't have to be you," June said in a measured tone. "There are other people who can do what your grandmother did, and they would be happy to step in if you needed them to. I'm sure of it. You only need to ask."

Alyssa frowned, trying to figure out whether June was alluding to the fact that Gran was a witch, or whether there was even more to Sylvie's role in the town that Alyssa wasn't aware of. She didn't know the older woman well enough to broach that topic just yet. A chill swept up her spine and all she wanted was to get rid of June, now, and lock the door, close the curtains, and shut the rest of the world out.

"Anyway," June said, breaking the silence which had stretched too long. "I brought you some chamomile tea, dear. You seemed a bit stressed the last time I saw you." She held the silver thermos out and Alyssa took it from her.

"Thanks," she said, not sure how she felt about the gesture. It was kind, though. She should be grateful. "I'll be sure to have some before I head to bed."

"Make sure you do. It will do you a world of good." June reached out and grasped Alyssa's arm, giving it a gentle squeeze. There was something almost possessive about the touch though, and Alyssa stood up straighter and stepped back into the house to put some distance between them.

"You moved the herb chest!" June exclaimed, pressing a hand to her neck. "What did you do that for?"

Alyssa spun to see what June was looking at, realising she was meaning an old chest Alyssa had dragged from the living room into the hallway to clear some space. She had no idea it contained herbs, but it seemed to weigh more than a miniature pony and had left grooves in the wooden flooring where she'd dragged it.

Better not let June see those...

"I was moving a few things around. You know, making the place mine," Alyssa said, emphasising the last word. The way June had brushed in here the other day, almost acting as if she belonged in the space, and her offense at Alyssa making changes was raising her hackles.

Where was Buttons when she needed him? He would no doubt hiss at the old woman the way that she wanted to.

"Yes, of course," June said, some of the heat leaving her voice. "It's just...Well, Sylvie was always so particular about things." She pursed her lips. "I don't suppose you've found the key for that chest, in your... decluttering, have you?"

"No," Alyssa said without thought. She hadn't, but she had a feeling that when she did, she wasn't going to be sharing that information with June.

"I'm sure it will turn up," June said with a tight

smile. She looked like she was going to reach out again, so Alyssa gripped the door, creating a barrier.

"Thanks so much for the tea," she said, forcing a warm smile and looking June right in the eyes. They locked gazes. June's sparked with something Alyssa couldn't quite decipher, but then the older woman gave a brief smile before turning and heading back down the path.

Alyssa watched until June was all the way off the property before she closed the door and locked it tight.

What was with that woman?

And what was she to Gran? Sylvie had never mentioned her in their weekly phone calls, but Alyssa was beginning to think there was a lot Gran hadn't mentioned.

She headed back to the lounge, slumping onto the couch and rubbing a hand over her face.

What the hell had Gran gotten her into?

Her gaze fell on the TV where she'd watched Gran's message the night before. The screen had gone blank, yes...but had there been more to follow? The recording hadn't properly finished, had it? Dread and curiosity warred in her gut as she reached forward, grabbed the remote, and hit play with a trembling finger.

Moments later, Gran's lined face filled the screen,

her blue eyes piercing even through the grainy film. "I needed to add more to the message, my dear," Gran said. "The ghost that haunts this house is no mere lost soul," she rasped. "He is a revenant, a malicious spirit. And he bears our family a terrible grudge."

Alyssa gripped a throw pillow hard enough to turn her knuckles white.

"Centuries ago, one of our ancestors was responsible for his death," Gran continued gravely. "A sorcerer in his own right, power-mad and cruel. Our many-times great grandmother, the first of us to settle here in Kotahi Bay, trapped his vengeful shade in a box, and confined that to this house. Bound him with blood and witchfire. And we, her daughters, have been his captors ever since."

On screen, Gran fixed the camera with a steely gaze. "It falls to you now, Alyssa. You must keep the binding strong, feed it with your own power, or risk him breaking free. Gaining a foothold in our world once more. You cannot allow that to happen."

The screen went black, leaving Alyssa gripping the pillow and struggling to breathe evenly. This was insane. She didn't want this responsibility! She didn't even feel like a real witch. Not anymore. Not since she'd made that vow to her teenage self...how was she supposed to contain an evil, centuries-old spirit?

But she couldn't just ignore it either. Not with the

warnings from both Gran and Mrs Nolan hanging over her head. She had to at least try.

Mind made up, Alyssa headed for the basement stairs, floorboards creaking under her slippers. In the secret room, she paged through the red grimoire until she found instructions on strengthening magical bindings. It didn't look too difficult. Some common herbs, a few drops of blood, an incantation. She could handle that.

A simple spell wouldn’t mean she was taking on the role of town witch, would it?

She gathered the necessary supplies, including dried thyme and sage from the kitchen, and set them out on Gran's workbench. Alyssa didn’t know what wood it was made from, but it had been well oiled; the scars from time and use were things of beauty rather than blemishes.

Her fingers trembled as she uncorked a vial of consecrated water and poured it into a copper bowl. The air felt thick, hard to breathe, and the shadows in the corners of the room seemed to deepen. The hair on the back of her neck stood up.

Alyssa shook herself and struck a match; the flame flickered and she couldn’t tear her eyes away from it, away from the memories. Heat seared her fingertips and she shook her hand. The flame died and she sucked on the fresh burns, the sting a vivid reminder of the past.

She had to focus. To be here. Now. She'd avoided thinking about that night for years now, she could keep avoiding it for a little longer.

Gran was counting on her. The town too, if Mrs Nolan was to be believed. She wished she had a lighter, but the ritual specifically called for matches; maybe the sulphur was a component of the spell too?

It didn't matter. What did, was to get this over and done with.

She lit the candles and began to recite the unfamiliar phrases, hoping her pronunciation wasn't too far off. She didn't know what the language was, but the words seemed to twist on her tongue, turning to ash in her mouth. The candles sputtered and died no matter how often she relit them. Sickly green smoke began to pour from the herbs, making her eyes water and her head spin.

Miri's face flashed before her eyes – the expression of terror – the flames – the screams...

Never again...No. More. Magic.

This was all wrong. Panic clawed at her throat as the candles went out again. She couldn't do this. She didn't have Gran's power, her iron will. The last time she'd tried a spell, her childhood best friend had ended up scarred and terrified. She couldn't do this.

She dumped the contents of her water bottle onto the smoking herbs and fled upstairs, Gran's grimoire clutched to her chest. Defeat sat bitter on her tongue.

Restless and filled with clawing unease, Alyssa paced the house, finding excuses to avoid the basement and its waiting shadows. She tried to focus on cleaning, on sorting through some of the clutter and boxed-up junk, but her mind kept circling back to the ghost. The revenant.

She needed to clear her head or she'd go mad. She headed to the café, hoping a strong coffee and some human interaction would settle her nerves.

The bell jingled cheerfully as she stepped inside the cosy space, breathing in the aroma of freshly-ground beans and baked goods. A tall man was already at the counter, dark hair, pale skin, and startling blue eyes that locked with hers when he turned to see who had come in. Alyssa averted her gaze, trying not to look like a weirdo for staring. He was drop dead gorgeous, in her eyes, anyway, but she wasn't ready to start something.

She made herself glance at the counter, noting a few posters stuck there, one promoting a 'magical' fair that was coming to town the next month. Maybe she would go. Alyssa ordered a flat white with a shot of vanilla, and a ham and cheese toasted sandwich from the older woman behind the counter, then found a table by the window, hands wrapped around the warm mug as she stared sightlessly out the window.

"Hey, Alyssa!"

The cheerful voice made her jump, sloshing coffee onto the polished wood tabletop. Alyssa looked up to see a stunning blonde settling into the chair across from her, blue eyes sparkling with mirth.

"I'm sorry, do I know you?" Alyssa asked warily, blotting up the spill with a napkin. She took in the woman's bright boho dress and beaded necklaces with a raised eyebrow. They were around the same age, but this woman seemed to have a world of wisdom that Alyssa felt she was lacking at the moment.

"Oh, honey, where are my manners? I'm Samantha. Sam to my friends." She stuck out an elegant hand weighed down with silver rings. Alyssa shook it. "We've met before, at the funeral, remember? I run the little curios shop down the way." Sam gestured further down the street, and Alyssa recalled looking in the window of the store and wondering whether they'd be willing to sell some of Gran's old things.

Alyssa smiled politely.

"I couldn't help but notice you looking a bit peaky," Sam said, leaning in with an air of conspiracy. "Anything you want to talk about?"

"I...no. Thank you." Alyssa looked down into her

mug, shoulders hunching. "It's just been a long few days."

"I bet." Samantha reached over and patted her wrist. Her expression was tinged with grief and understanding. "Losing Sylvie...she was a light in this town. Kept a lot of the old shadows at bay."

Alyssa's head snapped up, finally registering that Sam had said she was at the funeral too. "You knew my grandmother?"

Sam laughed. "Hon, everyone knew your grandmother. She was a force of nature." She fixed Alyssa with a piercing stare, a glint of mischief in her eyes. "From what I hear, you're cut from the same cloth. Even if you're only just realising it."

Alyssa shook her head, throat tightening. "I'm not...I can't be what she was. The magic...it's not for me. I only end up hurting people." Why was she confessing to having magic to this virtual stranger? She did her best to suppress the memories that flashed through her mind in jagged shards, but when she glanced out the window all she could see were flames and Miri's tormented face.

The incident still haunted her dreams. That terrible night...the acrid smell of smoke and— Alyssa shuddered and cut her thoughts off before they got any worse.

She'd turned her back on all that. Rejected her

power for fear of hurting anyone else. Gran had understood, even if the loss had carved fresh lines of grief into her face. She'd never pushed, never demanded Alyssa embrace her birthright. Not that her mother would have let her, even if she had wanted to. That summer had been the end of school holidays with Gran.

A warm hand covering hers jolted Alyssa back to the present. She looked up to see Sam watching her with gentle understanding.

"No one's asking you to be your grandmother," she said softly. "You've got to find your own way, your own strength. But don't turn your back on your gifts. They're a part of you." She squeezed Alyssa's hand before releasing it. "You can't trust everyone in this town. I'd steer clear of Mrs Nolan and the Council, if I was you."

Alyssa coughed. "Oh yeah...she visited me. Bad vibes."

Samantha nodded. "We don't really know what she's up to, but it doesn't feel natural. You need anything, you just let me know, okay? Us weird ones have to stick together."

With a wink and a flounce of gauzy skirts, Sam breezed out of the café, leaving Alyssa feeling oddly bereft. But there was a small spark of warmth in her chest now. A glimmer of belonging. Perhaps she could have friends here; she only hoped that they weren't conditional on her embracing magic.

On her way out of the café, Alyssa nearly collided with someone. She flinched and steadied the elderly woman, white plaits swinging as she propped herself on her carved walking stick.

"No need to rush," the woman said, eyes twinkling beneath deep lines that spoke of a lifetime of laughter. "The kawakawa won't fruit any faster for your hurrying."

"I'm sorry, I wasn't watching where—"

"You're Sylvie's girl." Not a question. She gestured to a free table. "I'm Constance. Your gran and I were the best of friends."

June had said much the same thing, but for some reason, Alyssa believed this earthy stranger more. There was something grounding about her presence, like the scent of rain-soaked soil.

"Join an old woman for a moment?" Constance said, gesturing to the outside table where potted herbs lined the railing, Alyssa noticed, the kinds Gran used to grow.

Despite her urge to flee, Alyssa found herself sitting. There was something about Constance that felt...steady. Unlike Mrs Nolan's demanding presence or June's cloying attention.

"This time of year, the horopito is at its strongest,"

Constance said, reaching to brush a leaf on the nearest plant. "Your grandmother understood its power – not just for healing, but for protection. All plants have their wisdom, if we remember how to listen. Papatūānuku speaks through them, guides us in their use."

Alyssa shifted uncomfortably. Here it came – another lecture about her heritage, about power and responsibility. "I'm not really into all that—"

"The land knows you," Constance continued. "Just as it knew your grandmother, and her mother before her. Some connections can't be denied, no matter how hard we try." She pulled a sprig of kawakawa from her basket, sliding it across the table. "For protection."

"Thank you, but—"

"We're having our summer Raumati celebration on Saturday," Constance said. "Your grandmother always helped lead the karakia." She held up a hand as Alyssa started to protest. "No pressure, dear. But you're welcome to come, be present. The earth remembers even when we forget."

"I appreciate the invitation, but I'm still settling in..." Alyssa glanced at the kawakawa leaf, fighting the urge to pick it up. She didn't know why she wanted to when most of her wanted to be alone right now, not hounded by every second townsperson. Still, something about this woman made her stop, and listen.

Constance nodded, unsurprised. "When you're ready then." She gathered her basket, patting Alyssa's hand as she stood. The touch felt warm.

Alyssa watched her go, the carved stick tapping the pavement. The kawakawa leaf sat innocently on the table, deep green and glossy. After a moment's hesitation, she tucked it into her pocket, telling herself it was just to be polite.

Still, as she walked home, feet scuffing on the salt-stained sidewalks, unease crept back in like a coastal fog. Gran's warnings echoed in her ears, Mrs Nolan's judgmental glower was giving her a headache. And then there were the terrors of the past, lurking behind the basement door like a coiled viper.

By the time she stepped back inside the house, Alyssa was ready to crawl out of her own skin. She eyed the door to the basement like it might burst open any minute, spilling necromantic horrors. How was she supposed to just go about her life with that hanging over her head?

Time for a change...

Alyssa grabbed some boxes from the laundry and headed to the lounge. She threw herself into work with a manic energy, as if she could shove away the creeping dread with the force of her determination to make this her home.

Back when she'd been a kid, she'd loved the old

'cottage' feel of the place, but now it was claustrophobic and she just wanted to declutter, start over. There was too much of Gran here, too much that hinted at things she could have known, but that had been stripped away from her when her mother barred Gran from their lives. She needed to see some change, and that was going to begin right here in the lounge.

Alyssa found some cardboard boxes in the laundry, probably from groceries, and grabbed a stack of newspapers that sat in a box by the fireplace. And then she packed away all the ornaments and figurines lining the mantle leaving only a few family portraits. Among them, curiously, was one of June and Gran standing close with their arms around each other's shoulders. There was something about the photo that made Alyssa think they had been more than just friends and neighbours.

She dumped that one in the box and then stripped the walls of their cross-stitch hangings and lame old paintings, leaving patches of vivid yellow paint marking the places where those items had once hung.

Anything with even the faintest hint of power behind it went into a separate box which she'd move to the basement just as soon as she could muster the courage. Knickknacks and doilies could all make their way to a charity store, and the stack of *Home and Living* magazines could go in the fire.

She busied herself for the rest of the day clearing out the things she didn't want, pushing furniture this way and that, removing pieces until she was happy. Why did old people always have so much furniture? Finally, she had a clean open space with minimal but comfortable seating. Now all it needed was a fresh coat of paint; but that could wait for tomorrow. The room looked a million times better already.

Slowly, bit by bit, the house was starting to look less like a musty old time capsule and more like a big blank canvas, ready for Alyssa to make her mark. She'd just wrestled Gran's ancient recliner over by the picture window when her phone rang, startling in the cloistered quiet.

It was Kelly. Alyssa answered with a breathless laugh, realising how hard she'd been working. And just how much she was missing her friend. "Hey, Kels."

"Don't you 'hey Kels' me!" her friend snapped, sounding frazzled. "I expected you back days ago! What's the deal?"

"I kind of...inherited a house?" Alyssa sank onto the windowsill. "Gran left me her place. I thought I'd stay on a bit. Fix it up."

"You're staying in Creepsville?" Kelly screeched,

making Alyssa wince and pull the phone away from her ear. "Are you insane?"

"It's not creepy," Alyssa said defensively. Then considered. "Okay, it's a little creepy. There may be a ghost."

Dead silence, then a sharp crackle of static as Kelly sighed. "Oh, for the love of...I'm coming down there. No way am I letting you deal with this solo. Besides, sounds like you could use a hand with the reno."

"Kels, you really don't have to—"

"Shut it. I'll be there tomorrow, and I expect a stocked bar and a juicy ghost story."

"Deal." Alyssa laughed, relief rushing through her. Kelly always knew how to put things in perspective. "You're the best."

"And don't you forget it. See you tomorrow, babe."

Alyssa tossed her phone on the couch, smile fading as her gaze fell on the door to the wooden box that she was sure she'd consigned to the donation bin.

Kelly's brash presence would be a welcome distraction, but it didn't change the truth. Alyssa was the mistress of this house now, and all its secrets. All its ghosts and shadows.

She couldn't outrun this legacy. This responsibility.

But maybe, just maybe, she wouldn't have to face it alone.

6

ALYSSA

Dinner was battered fish and perfectly deep-fried chips on the back porch with a glass of cheap Sauvignon Blanc. Pure class. The sun was still high, dappling the backyard through the well-established trees at the edges. There was no fence at the back, and the grass disappeared into low shrubs before becoming dense bush. About half of them were Pōhutukawa, their bushy crimson flowers in full bloom, the vibrant green leaves giving off the perfect New Zealand Christmas vibe; she really should try and put a tree up or something, but it didn't feel like Christmas with Gran gone.

They'd sat out here other summers, the pōhutukawa trees stretching their ancient limbs towards the sea, their red flowers blazing against dark leaves.

"The land remembers," Gran had said. "That's why we must respect it. Magic doesn't come from us – it comes through us, from the earth itself. From Papatūānuku, the earth mother, the great goddess who has always favored our line."

It was warm enough to swim even this late in the day if she'd had the urge to walk the few blocks to the sea; she could smell the salt on the breeze even here. But she didn't want to go there yet. Apart from the funeral, and a few trips to the local shops, she hadn't ventured out to see any of the sights of Kotahi Bay. All of her memories here were over a decade old and she wasn't prepared to make new ones until she'd decided whether to stick around.

On the one hand, it was a small town in the middle of nowhere, away from her friends and family. Her mother would probably never speak to her again if she lived in Gran's house – though she hadn't decided whether that was a pro or con – and her social life would no doubt die a quick, painless death.

On the other, she didn't have anything else in the world, apart from her good friend, Kelly. Alyssa had spent the last two years working in dead-end corporate jobs, living in London and missing home, trying to build a life with a man who didn't want her anymore. Tears pricked Alyssa's eyes as she thought about how she and Grant had moved back to New Zealand to start a family, but when that hadn't happened immediately and she'd sought medical advice, the news of her infertility had hit her hard.

Somehow, it had hit Grant even harder. He'd withdrawn from her emotionally, and as the days went by, their relationship had slipped away like ashes in the wind. When she'd finally confronted him, Grant said she wasn't the one for him. Not anymore. He wanted a family that she couldn't give him, not directly. Devastated, Alyssa had moved in with Kelly, who'd taken good care of her and encouraged her to cry her eyes out over many cheap bottles of wine and tubs of boysenberry ice cream.

This could be the fresh start she needed, an opportunity to set her life on a new path. There was nothing left for her anywhere else. There was nowhere she'd rather be, yet the skeletons in her family closet seemed a little too literal at this point, and then there were more practical considerations. She'd need to work to live, but a life without rent sounded pretty sweet right now, and the Bay had always been a beautiful place. It could be a good place to find that line between other people's hopes for her, and what she really wanted for herself.

Not to mention that she would never accidentally

bump into Grant here. Kotahi Bay was isolated, secluded, not exactly a tourist destination.

As she sat on the bench, watching the sun set through the leaves, her thoughts strayed to the secret room in the basement. She'd spent hours down there today, poring over Gran's books and notes, trying to make sense of the legacy that had been dumped on her shoulders.

The more she read, the more unsettled she became. Tales of scary sounding rituals and bizarre magic, spirits bound by force and will...It all seemed off.

And then there was the ghost itself. The revenant, as Gran called it. Alyssa still hadn't seen it properly, but she could feel its presence like a physical weight, oppressive and watchful. It set her teeth on edge and made her jump at shadows.

She wrapped up her leftovers and sculled the last of her wine. It wasn't very good, but she was used to drinking cheap alcohol.

Alyssa pushed to her feet, joints popping. The sun was painting the sky in vivid orange that faded to purple, but the beauty was lost on her now. She felt... uneasy. On edge. Like there was a storm brewing just over the horizon, dark clouds gathering in her periphery.

She couldn't put her finger on it, but something

had changed. A shift in the atmosphere, a crackling tension in the air. It set her nerves jangling, though nothing obvious had happened. It was like the whole town was holding its breath, waiting for the hammer to fall.

She didn't know what to make of Mrs Nolan's visit, or the way June kept popping up with vague warnings and cryptic advice. Alyssa didn't trust either of them, not fully, but she couldn't deny that they seemed to know more about this house, and her grandmother, than she did. She needed answers, needed to understand her role in all of this, but she needed to do it on her own terms.

Mind made up, Alyssa headed inside, determination thrumming in her veins. She'd go to the library tomorrow, see what she could dig up on the history of Kotahi Bay and its more...uncanny residents. And she'd pay a visit to Samantha's curio shop, see if the kind young blonde woman had any insight to offer.

One way or another, she was done being anyone else's puppet. It was time she started pulling her own strings.

Alyssa chucked the rubbish in the outside bin and went back into the house. Buttons escaped through the cat flap just moments after she closed the door, probably heading for any crumbs of fish. A chill swept over her, and she shivered as she refilled her wine glass. Her breath misted in the air and her eyes widened. "What the hell..."

Gran didn't have air conditioning, so there was no reason for this sudden influx of cold air. Not in the summer. Alyssa rushed through to the lounge and grabbed the blanket off the couch, swinging it around her shoulders as she moved through the house.

Could this be...?

"Hey, ghostie," Alyssa called out. "I'm not afraid of you!"

All the windows were shut, so where was that breeze coming from? She went up to the bedroom and checked the window there, but it was closed too. She watched the backyard, remembering her visitor from that first night, but there was no-one there now. Her breath fogged the glass. Well, some of it.

Alyssa stumbled back as she saw it.

The shape of a large hand was imprinted on the window in front of her. The wineglass slipped from her hand and shattered on the wooden floor, droplets of liquid splashing against her toes and up her calves.

"Whoa," she said, stepping back. Her feet were bare, and a sliver of glass cut into her skin. "Crap!" Her eyes flicked from the blood oozing onto the wood to the handprint still visible on the window. It wasn't just the air that was cold now, and her breath was trapped in her chest.

She no longer wanted to call out to the ghost, but still her mind raced, looking for a more logical explanation. "Maybe I touched it before. My hands are greasy from the chips...Yeah, that's it." Alyssa spoke the words aloud as though she were talking to herself, though her heart thudded, and she knew it was a lie. She just didn't want the nightmare to be real, and she certainly didn't want to let on to any potential ghost that she might be afraid. "Better get this cleaned up."

She winced as she hopped through to the bathroom, dragging Gran's first aid kit out, and removed the glass splinter from her foot with tweezers. She wrapped a bandage around it even though the wound was tiny, then she headed back to the bedroom with the dustpan and vacuum cleaner.

Apparently, the only thing worse than glass on the floor was having a ghost in the house. Despite the tremor in her hands, she had it cleaned up in no time. Alyssa grabbed an extra blanket from the bedroom, and a replacement glass of wine, then parked up on the couch.

There was nothing she wanted to watch, but that didn't matter. Any mindless drivel would do. Anything to make it seem like she was carrying on as normal. Just a woman hanging out in her totally ghost free house on a regular night of the week. Doing normal things.

Gran was still hooked up to broadcast television and there was something soothing about that. Alyssa found a channel showing the annual Christmas in the Park concert, turned it up loud, and let the cheery carols, sung by local celebrities and pop stars, flood the lounge.

But even as she sat there, swaddled in blankets with her liquid courage firmly in hand, Alyssa couldn't shake the cloying unease, the sense that something was coming. The air seemed to hum with it, sly and insidious, curling around her ankles like a creeping fog.

Buttons jumped up beside her, startling a yelp from her throat. The cat just stared at her, inscrutable, before curling into a tight ball, his fur bristling. He seemed agitated, wary. Feeding off her own nervous energy.

Alyssa clutched her wine glass tighter, knuckles bleeding white. She wasn't ready for this. Wasn't strong enough, wise enough, magic enough. She'd tried the spell Gran had talked about and it had all gone wrong. Perhaps she was cursed to ruin the family legacy rather than save it. Had Gran been naïve in leaving it all up to her?

But ready or not, the shadows were gathering. The storm was closing in.

And one way or another, she'd have to find a way to weather it.

7

ALYSSA

Alyssa groaned as the pounding on the front door reverberated through her skull, amplifying the throbbing behind her eyes. She sat up gingerly, the rough wool of the couch scratching her bare legs. A shaft of late morning sunlight speared through a gap in the heavy drapes, making her wince.

"I'm never drinking again," she vowed, voice raspy. Her tongue felt like sandpaper and tasted about as pleasant. Buttons mrroewed indignantly as she staggered to her feet, though he stayed firmly on the couch despite the fact she thought he'd been sleeping on her chest. A glance down confirmed she was still in yesterday's rumpled sundress, now creased beyond saving. There was no time to do anything about that right now though.

The knocking resumed, loud and insistent. Alyssa shuffled to the door, one hand pressed to her temple. She squinted against the dazzling sunshine as she twisted the handle, shading her eyes with her other hand.

June beamed at her from the stoop, bright eyed and bushy tailed and far too chipper for— Alyssa glanced at her bare wrist, then remembered she'd removed her watch some time after the third glass of wine last night. It had to be mid-morning, at least. Unless the older woman main-lined coffee first thing.

Coffee. She could really do with one. With a shot of hazelnut.

"Alyssa, dear! I thought I'd pop by with some more fresh muffins, see how you're settling in." June brandished another wicker basket, the sweet scent of blueberries and lemon zest wafting out from under the red gingham cloth.

Before Alyssa could muster a response beyond a grunt, the older woman brushed past her, marching down the hall towards the kitchen like she owned the place. Alyssa scowled at her retreating back. June wore white capri pants and an airy lavender blouse that fluttered as she walked, her silvery hair perfectly coiffed. She looked like she'd stepped out of some TV ad for adult diapers or life insurance.

Buttons took one look at the interloper and bolted

for the cat flap, his tail lashing. Alyssa watched him go with envy. If only she could flee from social interaction so easily.

In the kitchen, June set her basket on the table with a flourish, the heels of her pristine white sandals clacking on the linoleum. She turned to Alyssa with a smile that didn't quite reach her eyes. "I know it's early, but I just couldn't wait. I wanted to check in to see how you were doing. Do you need anything?"

Alyssa leaned against the counter and folded her arms, the chill of the Formica seeping through her thin dress. "I'm fine," she said shortly. "Still adjusting. You know how it is." She waved a hand, then immediately regretted it as the motion made her head swim. Had she really drunk that much? She'd thought the chamomile tea she'd had before she passed out would help hydrate her, but she felt so much worse than she should.

June tutted, looking Alyssa up and down. Her gaze lingered on the wine stain near the hem of Alyssa's dress, the bird's nest of her hair. "Of course, dear. I imagine this has all been quite the...challenge."

There was an undertone to the words Alyssa didn't care for, a blend of condescension and gleeful schadenfreude. She straightened, tugging the dress down her thighs. "I'm managing," she said coolly. "But where are my manners? Let me get you a cup of tea."

She busied herself filling the kettle, glad for the distraction but very aware of June's hawkish gaze on her back as made tea in the rose-patterned teapot Gran had always saved for guests. The ritual soothed her, as did the growing rushing sound of the kettle, but her head continued to throb dully behind her eyes.

"So kind of you to check on me," Alyssa said as she carried the tea tray to the table, the words only slightly barbed. "I'd have thought you had better things to do."

"Nonsense," June trilled, picking up the delicate teacup painted with violets. "Nothing is more important than ensuring you feel welcome and supported. Especially with your gran...gone."

She paused expectantly, eyes gleaming, like she expected Alyssa to crumple at the mention of Sylvie. When Alyssa merely sipped her tea, June forged on. "I've spent so much time in this house over the years, you know. It feels like a second home. I'm sure you understand."

Alyssa fixed a vague smile on her face. "Of course."

June leaned back in her chair, cup cradled in her manicured hands. Her nails were the same shade as her top, Alyssa noted, distracted by the glint of her heavy silver rings as her fingers flexed. Was this woman always so put together? Alyssa might have been younger, had less wrinkles, but she felt frumpy next to June.

"It warms my heart to see you settling in so well," June said, and there again was that note in her voice, sly and faintly mocking. Like she knew something Alyssa didn't. "Though of course, no one would blame you if small town life proved...challenging after the bright lights of the city."

Alyssa's temple throbbed. June's voice seemed to scrape against her raw nerves, setting her teeth on edge. She took a fortifying gulp of her tea, eyes watering as it scalded her tongue. She wanted to kick June out, but it seemed rude when she and Gran had been close friends.

Forcing a bright smile, Alyssa said, "You're so thoughtful, but I'm tougher than I look. I'm sure I'll adapt in no time."

June hummed, gaze calculating. "Of course you will, dear." It sounded like a challenge.

They sipped their tea in silence for a long, excruciating moment. Alyssa's stomach gurgled loudly and she realised she hadn't eaten since...God, she couldn't even remember. She eyed June's muffin basket, her mouth watering despite the nausea churning in her gut.

As if reading her mind, June nudged the basket towards her. "Please, dear, help yourself. You look a bit peaky. My blueberry muffins are just the thing to perk you up."

Gratefully, Alyssa plucked a muffin from the basket, the top studded with glistening berries. She took a large bite, her eyes fluttering shut as buttery crumbs melted on her tongue, the muffin still warm from June's kitchen. She swallowed, then took another bite, larger than the first.

"There's a dear," June cooed. "Nothing like some home baking to settle the stomach and soothe the soul."

Alyssa could only nod, her cheeks bulging. She chased the muffin with a swig of tea, the hot liquid washing away the cloying sweetness.

June set down her cup with a decisive clink. "Well, I should be going. I'm sure you have a busy day ahead, getting the house sorted and all." Her eyes cut to the stacks of boxes cluttering the room, the bare walls where Gran's cluttered collections of art and nostalgic kiwiana used to hang, tutting under her breath.

Alyssa followed her gaze, something tightening in her chest. The house did look bare, cold even, shorn of Gran's knickknacks and doilies. But it was Alyssa's now. Hers to make into a home, to build a life. Even if she had no earthly idea how to go about it.

“You haven’t happened upon a box, have you?” June asked. Her tone was casual, but a sliver of tension shot through Alyssa with the question. "It's about this big." June gestured with her hands. "Has some symbols etched into it. I left it here and would love to get it back."

Alyssa shook her head and hoped she could pull off a lie. "No, not yet. When I find it, I'll be sure to let you know though." She could practically feel the box vibrating from the living room, and just had to hope that the woman wouldn't notice it sitting on the coffee table as she left.

With that thought, she stood. "I should really get back to things, but thank you so much for the muffins and the check in." June took the hint and stood as well, brushing invisible crumbs off her lap as she did. She raised an eyebrow and Alyssa realised she was waiting for the basket, so she scooped out the remaining muffins and put them on a plate.

Alyssa walked June to the door, making sure to cover the view into the living room with her body as they passed that door. She wasn't sure why, but the urge was too strong to avoid.

"You really haven't seen that box, have you?" June asked. Her tone was casual, but a spike of unease shot through Alyssa.

"No, I can't say that I have. I'll keep an eye out for it though."

On the threshold, June paused, looking back at

Alyssa with an unreadable expression. "I know Sylvie had high hopes for you. For your...role here." Her eyes seemed to bore into Alyssa's, dark and intent. "If you ever need guidance, my door is always open. Day or night."

With that vaguely ominous pronouncement, she clacked down the steps, sandals flashing in the harsh noon light. Alyssa watched her go, a prickle of unease running down her spine. June's words felt weighted, weighted in a way that had nothing to do with neighbourly concern.

High hopes. What was that supposed to mean? And what role? Did June know about the witch stuff? Alyssa's head spun with questions, each more troubling than the last. She thought of the ghost – revenant, Gran had called it – lurking in the depths of the house, somewhere. The way Gran's voice had rasped with urgency on the tape, impressing the importance of Alyssa's 'duty'.

Suddenly, the warm sweetness of the muffin turned sour in her mouth. She needed answers, needed to understand what exactly she'd been dropped into. June clearly knew more than she was saying, but Alyssa instinctively shied from seeking her counsel again. There was something about the woman that raised her hackles, some glint of menace in her eyes when she looked around Gran's house.

No, if Alyssa wanted the truth – about Gran, about whatever lurked in this town – she needed an unbiased source. Someone without an agenda.

Her mind flashed to Samantha, the warm, effusive woman from the curio shop who said she'd known Gran. Perhaps she could shed some light on the secrets that seemed to whirl around Alyssa like an icy wind.

Alyssa headed for the stairs to shower and change. The pounding in her head had lessened to a manageable ache and she felt more human and functional than she had earlier.

8

ALYSSA

Thirty minutes later Alyssa stepped out into the blinding sunlight. Summer was ramping up and the pōhutukawa trees were in full bloom. Native birds were chirping happily, flitting between the trees, some of them darting through the air to snack on the bugs she kicked up as she walked. She'd put on an emerald green sundress in an attempt to feel kind of put together, with strappy sandals to complete the look, and a swipe of lip gloss. It was the most effort she'd made in a long time.

The curio shop was only a few blocks from Gran's – her – house, nestled between the post office and a tiny used bookstore. A weathered sign above the deep green door proclaimed it 'Sage & Salt'. Alyssa frowned up at it for a long moment, worrying her bottom lip between her teeth.

Through the plate glass window, she could see crystals and wind chimes and long swaths of gauzy fabric, all artfully draped and displayed like some Stevie Nicks fever dream. It looked like exactly the kind of place her mother had always railed against, deriding it as "New Age hogwash".

But then, her mother had turned her back on her own mother, on their heritage, so bitterly and completely that she'd forbidden Alyssa from even mentioning Gran. Her mother was pushy and mean and manipulative as well, so her judgment didn't count for much.

Suddenly, she caught sight of herself in the window reflection and drew back in surprise.

Things were worse than she'd imagined. Her hair was long and raggedy, and even after she'd dragged a brush through it this morning, it still looked unkempt. And she was walking around like this?

No. Something had to be done. Now.

Alyssa kept walking, hoping that there was a salon somewhere along this street. It was basically the only street with businesses on it, so surely...

There. She spotted a sign with a pair of scissors on it, and the name 'Tricks and Tresses', across the street and headed towards it, pushing the door open before she could overthink it. A bell tinkled and the hairdresser turned away from a man who sat in front of a mirror. No one looks good in those black hair-catching capes, Alyssa thought to herself, even this guy, who should theoretically be attractive.

"Be with you in a moment, doll," they called.

Alyssa didn't want to presume pronouns in this case, because the hairdresser's style defied gender norms. She took a seat in the waiting area and grabbed a magazine, flicking through it without actually taking anything in. Instead, her gaze moved around the room, taking in the limited number of stations dotting the floor. Maybe she should just leave, but she couldn't slip out the door without it being obvious. No crowd to get lost in here in the Bay; and she'd never be able to come in the salon again if she bolted now.

Before she knew it, the man was standing up and heading to the counter. He was tall, with dark hair and tattoos on both his forearms, and no doubt some other places as well.

"Hey, you're Alyssa, right?" He asked the question as he moved towards the counter to pay.

"That's me! Is there some kind of town newsletter with daily updates or something?" The question came out half-jokingly, half concerned. Everyone seemed to know who she was, but she knew no one and that made her feel...squirmy.

"Small towns," he said with a wry smile. "I'm Matai." He held out a hand for her to shake. His fingers were warm in hers and while he looked a little intimidating, she didn't get any bad feelings from the guy. "See you around, no doubt." He tipped his head at her and then moved towards the door.

"He's our local tattoo artist," the hairdresser said. "In case you're in the market for some ink." They gave her an assessing look. "But I think you're here because you need a little tidy up, right?"

"It's fairly obvious," she said with a wry smile. "I've been...busy." Or distracted, grieving, too caught up in her own misery to look in the mirror for long enough, or to realise just how bad things had gotten.

"Then you're in the right place, lovely. Come back here." They beckoned her into a chair and whisked a black cape around her, fastening it at the nape of her neck. "I'm Quinn by the way, and I'm going to make you feel like a brand new person."

"If you can do that, then you might just be a magician," she said, only half joking. What was it about being sat in a chair with a cloak around you that made everyone look so bad? Her skin was far too pale, and blotchy as well; the bags under her eyes were bigger than the one she'd packed to come to the Bay.

"Trust me. You'll feel amazing by the time I'm done, so might as well start now." They cocked one hip as they feathered their fingers over her hair. "Do you have anything in mind, or do you just want me to..."

They locked eyes in the mirror and Alyssa felt herself relax. She was in good hands. She could feel it. She'd had to make too many decisions lately, or had too many still to make, and she didn't know what she wanted right now.

"Do your magic," she said with a firm nod. And maybe it was a kind of magic because they put some soft tunes on in the background, spent some time massaging her scalp, working some delicately scented oil into her head, and then seemed to become a whirling dervish the likes of which she'd not seen since watching Edward Scissorhands, and the end result was just as impressive.

Quinn had lopped off the length, giving Alyssa a mid-length shaggy bob that somehow made her blonde locks more vibrant and glossier than they'd ever been before. She gasped and reached up to touch them.

"How did you make my hair so...good?"

"It's better than good, honey, it's dee-vine. You're a goddess in waiting." Quinn put their tools down on the counter and then squirted something else onto their hands before scrunching the product through her hair, somehow making the natural wave look styled rather than birds-nest. The end effect was better than any high-priced salon she'd ever gone to in the city.

"You are a magician," Alyssa said. She bit her lip as she looked at her reflection. It was so different to the way she'd looked in the window of Sage & Salt. Would Samantha even recognise her? Did Alyssa recognise herself?

No, she did. There was something about the style that was freeing. A return of something that had been missing for so many years. Something she couldn't place her finger on.

"Thank you so much." She stood up once they'd removed the cape. "Can I hug you?"

"I'd be offended if you didn't," Quinn said. They opened their arms and Alyssa stepped into them. The embrace was warm, welcoming, and she realised that it had been far too long since anyone had held her, and now this perfect stranger was cradling her like Alyssa's mother should have at the news of Gran's death. Tears pricked her eyes, but she shoved them down, not wanting to burden this wonderful human being who had made her whole day better.

When she pulled away, she had to turn towards

the counter, giving herself just a few seconds to pull her features into something a little less sentimental.

"How much do I owe you?" she asked.

"First time is free for new residents," they said, giving her a wink.

"But I don't know if I'm staying..."

Quinn looked her up and down and nodded. "I've got a good feeling about you, so if it makes you feel better, we can say it's because you're Sylvie's granddaughter, okay?"

Alyssa frowned. Not knowing if she was comfortable with what felt like such a huge gift. They might have considered it a simple haircut, but it was so much more to her. "Are you sure?"

"Most definitely," Quinn replied. "Besides, you're going to walk out that door and tell all your friends about this fabulous little salon in Kotahi Bay." They winked at her, then ushered her towards the door. "Have a good day!"

Alyssa stood on the sidewalk for a moment, watching as Quinn went to tidy up. She couldn't quite believe her luck, and as tempted as she was to leave her concerns on the salon floor with the rest of her hair, she knew she couldn't head home until she'd done what she came to do and asked Samantha for advice.

Drawing in a deep, steadying breath, Alyssa

pushed open the door to Sage & Salt. A bell tinkled merrily above her head. Instantly, she was engulfed by the heady scent of incense, something sweet and spicy that made her nose twitch. The shop was dim and cool after the brightness of the street, a balm to her sun-dazzled eyes.

"Be with you in just a moment!" a warm and slightly muffled voice called from the back.

Alyssa drifted deeper into the shop, trailing her fingers along the smooth edges of the crystals and geodes that lined the shelves. They seemed to hum beneath her touch, resonating against her skin like struck tuning forks. She jerked her hand back, startled.

"Alyssa Whenua! What a pleasant surprise!"

Alyssa turned to see Samantha emerging from behind a beaded curtain, arms spread wide in welcome, bangles jingling. Today she wore a flowing turquoise caftan over baggy jeans, her feet bare. Her smile was bright.

"Hi, Samantha," Alyssa said, her own smile feeling stiff and forced. "I hope I'm not intruding."

"Never, and it looks like you've visited our local salon. Love the new hair. Quinn is a genius, aren't they?" Samantha said, grinning as she came out from behind the counter to clasp Alyssa's hands. Her skin was soft and cool, her grip strong. "I'm always happy to see a friendly face. Especially one so closely tied to Sylvie."

"Actually, that's why I'm here," she said, the words tumbling out in a rush before she could second guess them. "I was hoping you could...shed some light on a few things."

Samantha's eyes crinkled at the corners, her smile softening. She gave Alyssa's hands a squeeze before releasing them. "Let me guess. Our little town is proving more mysterious than you bargained for?"

Alyssa let out a shaky laugh. "You could say that." She glanced around, taking in the hanging herbs and softly glowing lanterns, the little piles of smooth stones and dried flowers. "I feel like I've landed in an episode of *The Twilight Zone*."

"Mmm, Kotahi Bay has that effect on people," Samantha agreed, a glint of mirth dancing in her eyes. "Especially those with a sensitivity to the hidden currents."

Alyssa's brow furrowed. "Sensitivity?"

Samantha waved a hand airily. "Oh, you know. A certain attunement to the energies that flow through this place. The magic."

She said it so casually, like commenting on the weather. Alyssa felt a frisson run through her, electric and unsettling. "Magic," she repeated flatly. She'd been running from that word for so many years. If she was being completely honest, this was the real reason she hadn't visited. She'd missed Gran so much, but it was hard to separate the trauma of the past – the horrible incident that still tortured her – from this place.

"Kotahi Bay is magic," Alyssa said, her own voice sounding foreign to her.

Samantha laughed, the sound like bells pealing. "Surely you've felt it, Alyssa. In your blood, your bones. This town, it recognises you. Welcomes you. This is where you belong."

Alyssa wanted to deny it. Magic was dangerous. There was too much dark potential, and yet...there was the strange and beautiful humming of the crystals. The way the salt air seemed to crackle against her skin sometimes, heavy with intent. The hair on the back of her neck stood up.

Samantha was watching her closely, gaze knowing. "You have questions," she said gently. "About your grandmother. About her role in this place, and the... responsibility she left you."

Alyssa's heart stuttered, a cold sweat breaking out along her hairline. "How did you..."

"Oh, honey. Sylvie was one of my dearest friends. She and Constance have done their best to protect the bay, and now it's up to the younger generations to help. Your Gran knew this day would come. That you would come."

Alyssa didn't know what to say to all that. She simply smiled and nodded as Samantha took her elbow, steering her towards a little curtained alcove. Samantha drew aside the gauzy drape to reveal two plump armchairs, a low table set between them bearing a steaming teapot and two cups, pale green and translucent as sea glass.

“How did you know?” Alyssa asked.

“It's funny. I had a feeling someone was coming in, someone who needed to chat," Samantha said, directing Alyssa into one of the chairs, settling across from her and busying herself pouring the fragrant tea. It smelled herbaceous and slightly sweet, like mint and honey.

Alyssa wrapped her fingers around the delicate cup, letting the warmth seep into her hands. She was suddenly fiercely grateful for Samantha's gentle guidance, the serene hush of the little sanctuary she'd created.

"So," Samantha said after a moment. "What is it you want to know?"

Alyssa swallowed hard, the questions that had been burning in her throat suddenly lodged there, choking her. She took a sip of tea to ease the tightness, the subtle sweetness coating her tongue.

When she found her voice, it emerged small and unsteady. "The ghost," she said, the word like ashes in her mouth. "The...revenant. What is it? Why is it... why is it my problem all of a sudden?"

Samantha sighed, settling deeper into her chair. She cradled her own teacup just below her chin, the wisps of steam curling around her face like spectral fingers.

"I don't know that much about the spirit because Sylvie was awfully cagey when it came to family secrets. I do know that it's old, Alyssa. Very old, and very angry. It's been bound to your family for generations, passed down from mother to daughter like a cursed heirloom."

Alyssa shuddered, Gran's urgent words from the video echoing in her mind. The weight of them settled on her shoulders like a lead cape, heavy and smothering.

"But why?" she asked hoarsely. "Why us? What did we do to deserve this...this burden?"

Samantha's smile was sad, almost pitiful. "Oh, honey. You didn't do anything. This is so much bigger than you."

She leaned forward, fixing Alyssa with an intent gaze. "The women of your line...you're special, Alyssa. Powerful. You have a connection with the unseen, an ability to connect with the magic of this earth. It's in your blood."

Alyssa shrank back in her chair, shaking her head even as some deep, hidden part of her resonated with the truth of Samantha's words. Miri's scream echoed in her mind, the smell of singed flesh and hair suddenly choking.

Her power had surged out of control and poor, innocent Miri had been hurt. There was no going back – no changing the past. Miri was out there somewhere, perhaps still grappling with that night long ago, or perhaps she'd moved on. Alyssa didn't know how to move on...

The memory crashed over her with visceral clarity: Fourteen years old, showing off for her best friend in Gran's garden. They'd been practicing simple spells all summer – lighting candles with a thought, making flowers bloom out of season. Miri had been fascinated, begging to learn more. Gran had always warned her not to play with fire.

"Just a little fire," Miri had pleaded. "Show me how you make those coloured flames you told me about!"

Alyssa had been so confident, drunk on power and teenage certainty. She'd reached for the magic, feeling it surge through her veins like lightning. But something went wrong. The spark she'd meant to create exploded into an inferno, wild and hungry. Miri's sleeve caught first. Then her hair....

Gran had appeared seemingly out of nowhere, containing the flames with a wave of her hand. But the damage was done. Miri's screams still echoed in Alyssa's nightmares, along with the acrid smell of burned hair and flesh, the sight of angry red burns spreading across her friend's skin.

She'd lost control, and someone she loved had paid the price.

That night, she'd sworn off magic forever. Locked that part of herself away so thoroughly she'd almost convinced herself it had never existed. Almost.

Gran had managed to contain the damage, but Alyssa had sworn off magic then and there. The guilt still gnawed at her. Gran had insisted it wasn't her fault, that she just needed to learn control, but Alyssa couldn't risk hurting anyone else she loved.

"No," she said, voice cracking. "I'm not...I can't be what you say. The last time I tried to tap into...into whatever this is..." She swallowed convulsively, eyes burning. "People got hurt. I got hurt. I won't risk that again."

"I know you're frightened," Samantha said. "I can feel that you've been running from this part of yourself for a long time. But Alyssa...you can't outpace destiny. And this town, this legacy...it's yours.

Whether you like it or not." The words felt like a slap, though Samantha's voice could not have been gentler.

Alyssa closed her eyes, hot tears leaking from beneath her lashes. She felt heard, seen, in a way she hadn't been in years. Not since Gran...

Gran. The thought of her was a fist around Alyssa's heart. She'd been so strong, so certain. She'd never shied away from her power, her purpose. And she'd thought Alyssa could bear that same mantle.

But Gran had been wrong before. Could she be wrong about this too?

"What if I can't do it?" Alyssa asked, voice small and wavering. "What if I fail? This revenant, whatever it is...I'm not strong enough to contain it. I tried and it all went wrong and now I'm scared I'm going to set it loose to wreak havoc."

Samantha reached over and squeezed Alyssa's hand. "You are so much more than that, Alyssa Whenua," she said firmly. "You are the daughter of witches, the heiress to a legacy of power and protection. Magic is your birthright. As for the revenant...you're stronger than you know, and you're not alone."

She released Alyssa's hands and sat back, taking a long sip of her tea. "I can teach you what you need to know. Help you develop your gifts. And when the time comes..."

Relief crashed over Alyssa like a wave, so acute it

left her light-headed. She slumped back in her chair, boneless, the teacup trembling in her grasp.

"Thank you," Alyssa whispered, the words choked and inadequate. "I don't...I can't..."

"No need for thanks," said Samantha. "And it's not just me. There are plenty of friends here in the Bay. You just need to get to know them."

And for the first time since she'd set foot back in Kotahi Bay, the tight knot of dread in Alyssa's chest began to loosen. She felt lighter, buoyed by a cautious hope.

"Remember," Samantha said, holding Alyssa's gaze intently. "You are stronger than you know. Braver than you believe. Trust your instincts, and trust in your heritage."

A breeze kicked up as Alyssa left the shop, whipping her hair around her face, tugging playfully at the skirt of her sundress. It carried the scent of salt and seaweed, of sunbaked sand and spices.

Magic, she thought, a giddy thrill running through her. The magic of Kotahi Bay. The magic that ran in her very veins. It seemed to sing to her now, rising with the wind, playful and enticing.

Come, it seemed to say. Come and play. Come and be what you were always meant to be.

And for the first time, Alyssa felt herself lean into it, into the pull, the yearning for more than the ordinary. She had loved magic, so, so much, so long ago, before everything had gone wrong. Before she'd played with fire – literally – and her friend had gotten burned.

But that was a long time ago.

With a deep, shuddering breath, Alyssa began to walk, her steps lighter than they'd been in years.

Voices carried on the evening air as Alyssa took the long way home. From the park, she could see gatherers on the hillside – circles of people around small fires, the scent of hāngi rising from the earth oven. Karakia mingled with guitar music, and children played among the pōhutukawa trees strung with fairy lights.

She hesitated at the edge of the park. There was an empty chair, draped with a familiar shawl. Gran's shawl...Beyond it, Constance sat with her eyes closed, swaying slightly as she led a chant that seemed to make the very ground hum.

Something pulled at Alyssa's chest – recognition, longing, fear. Not yet. She wasn't ready. But maybe someday...it would be time to stop running.

9

SAMANTHA

Samantha traced sigils in the condensation on her shop window, watching rain bead down the glass. The symbols glowed faintly – not enough for mundane eyes to notice, but a witch would see. A witch like Alyssa Whenua, if she properly remembered who she was.

The bell above the door chimed. Matai's presence filled the shop, bringing with it the scent of petrichor and something darker – ink and blood and magic worked into skin.

"You felt it too?" he asked, shrugging off his wet jacket.

Samantha nodded, not turning from the window. “Another tremor...The barrier trembled when Sylvie passed. It's weaker now." She pressed her palm flat against the glass. "Constance is powerful, but..."

"But she's one witch trying to hold back the tide." Matai moved beside her, rolling up his sleeves. Fresh tattoos spiraled up his forearms, not yet fully healed. Protection runes, binding spells, honoring and entreating the gods of this land.

"The old guard is failing," Samantha said softly. "Constance tries, but her magic is bound to the old ways. She can't adapt fast enough. I'm doing what I can to help..."

"And the new blood?" The question hung heavy between them.

Samantha thought of Alyssa, of the raw power she'd sensed beneath the girl's grief and denial. "Untested. Untrained." She paused. "Afraid of magic."

"Can't blame her, after what happened." Matai traced one of his tattoos absently. "Fire magic is tricky. Dangerous."

Sylvie had told them of Alyssa's hesitation, of her resistance to magic, but she'd had such unshakeable faith that her granddaughter would find her way.

"We don't have time for fear." Samantha turned finally, meeting his eyes. "Tu grows stronger. The others might not see it, but I do. The signs are there – in the way the tides change, in how the land itself seems to hold its breath."

Matai's expression darkened. "The gods have their own battles to wage. We're just caught in between."

"And the barrier is all that keeps their war from spilling into our world." Samantha moved to the counter, pulling out her ledger. Old names filled its pages, a record of power passed down through generations. She found Sylvie's name, still glowing faintly. Beside it, Alyssa's name had appeared the moment she'd crossed the town line. "Sylvie believed her granddaughter could help to anchor the barrier."

"But you haven't told her yet."

"No, "Sam said. "She's not ready, but I believe in her too. She's strong. She could be just what we need."

"Or she could bring it all down around us." Matai ran a hand through his rain-damp hair. "You've seen how the magic responds to her – power can be dangerous..."

"Perhaps that's exactly what we need." Samantha smiled, but there was an edge to it. "The old ways aren't working anymore. Maybe it's time for something new. Something wild."

"The others won't like it. Especially not Mrs Nolan."

"The others don't have to like it. They just have to survive it." Samantha closed the ledger with a snap. "Besides, they don't know what we know. About what's really happening beyond the barrier."

Matai was quiet for a long moment. "We should tell her. Alyssa. She deserves to know what she's walking into."

"Not yet." Samantha's fingers traced the edge of the ledger. "Let her find her feet first. Let her remember who she is, what magic feels like. Then..."

"Then we tell her we've been waiting for her? That her grandmother's death wasn't exactly natural? That there are things in this town older and darker than a Viking ghost?"

Samantha's lips curved. "We tell her what she needs to know. When she needs to know it." She looked out the window again, to where the barrier shimmered just beyond mortal sight. "For now, we watch. We wait. And we pray she's strong enough for what's coming."

The shop's crystals hummed in response, a discordant note that set Samantha's teeth on edge. Change was coming to Kotahi Bay, whether they were ready or not.

10

ALYSSA

Alyssa returned to the house, laden with paint and supplies; she dumped them all on the lounge floor and surveyed the room. This was going to be where she spent the most time, so it was important to get it right. Currently, it was a faded yellow. Oh, how she hated that musty old yellow paint. It was the most hideous thing in the entire world and she was going to abolish it with a warm white and a feature wall of vibrant teal-blue around the fireplace.

She took down the remaining pictures and dusted the sills with a cloth before heading to the mantle with some painter's tape.

And there was the box, the one that June wanted. Alyssa lifted it carefully and turned it over in her hands. It was cool to the touch, and she could now vividly remember placing it in a box along with the rest of the stuff. So how the hell had it found its way back here?

Freaking weird. Maybe the ghost had been playing tricks on her? She shrugged it off as best she could and took it into the kitchen with the other things she had decided to keep and left it on the table there. She would have to find June later and let her know it had turned up. At least that was one less thing to think about. It could do all the disappearing tricks it wanted in June's house.

As she set the box down, Alyssa's gaze drifted to the basement door. The secret room lurked below, filled with Gran's arcane treasures and witchy paraphernalia. A shiver ran down her spine as she recalled the musty scent of old leather-bound tomes, the glint of strange symbols etched into silver amulets, jars of herbs and powders with faded, inscrutable labels. Part of her itched to explore further, to delve into the mysteries hidden there. But a larger part recoiled, memories of scorching heat and screams echoing in her mind. She clenched her fists, pushing the thoughts away. No. She wouldn't risk touching that power again, no matter how alluring it might seem.

A sharp knock interrupted Alyssa's cleaning.

Through the frosted glass, she could make out Derek McDermott's reedy silhouette.

Her stomach dropped – what now?

"Miss Whenua!" The lawyer's too-bright smile didn't reach his eyes. "I was just passing by. Thought I'd check how you're settling in."

Just passing by? The house wasn't on the way to anywhere in particular.

"I'm fine, thanks." She didn't open the door fully. "Still sorting things out around here."

"Of course, of course." He shifted from foot to foot, neck craning to see past her into the house. "Found anything...interesting in your grandmother's belongings?"

"Not really." The lie came easily. "Mostly old furniture, photos."

"Ah." Was that disappointment? "Well, if you do find anything unusual – documents, artifacts, anything that seems...significant – I'd be happy to help evaluate them. As your grandmother's lawyer, I have certain...responsibilities."

There was an eagerness in his tone that set her teeth on edge.

"Err...I'll keep that in mind."

"Please do." He pulled out a business card, pressing it into her hand. The paper felt oddly warm, almost vibrating. "Day or night. Any time at all."

As she watched him walk away, something seemed off about him. The business card tingled against her palm. She dropped it in the bin. Maybe he was a bargain hunter looking for top quality antiques at low prices. That might explain his enthusiasm.

And now, to paint. There was nothing more rewarding than making something your own, not that she'd had much experience of that, having moved too many times to count and never having owned a place. She did, however, remember that time her mother had let her pick the paint colour for her bedroom, just after she'd banned her from seeing Gran. Alyssa had chosen black, everywhere, with glow in the dark stars on the ceiling. Her mother had frowned and folded her arms, but let her go ahead with it. Small price to pay, apparently.

The preparation felt like it took longer than the actual painting, but before too long she had the base coat of white, eradicating that sickly yellow hue, banishing it to bygone years. The entire space seemed bigger, cleaner, brighter. For the first time since arriving, joy overwhelmed grief.

The mid-afternoon sunlight streamed through the main window, pooling on the couch in the middle of the room. Even covered, it looked appealing and she could see herself there, some other day, sitting in the sun, reading a book with a bottle of beer resting on the floor beside her.

Yeah, she could see herself here, in this house, this town. It was different to how she might have imagined her life, sure, but she could make it a home. A home that was already filled with warmth and love, left over from the years that Gran had lived here.

As she took the tray and roller outside to wash, her phone rang loudly, vibrating across the mantelpiece until it hit the box. What the...She'd definitely taken that to the kitchen, hadn't she? She reached for the phone, noting that it was Kelly as she swiped to accept the call. "Hey, Kels! Where are you?"

She tucked the phone between her shoulder and ear and grabbed her tools, heading through the kitchen with them.

"I'm trying to find this godforsaken town of yours. How the hell do I get there?" Kelly sounded righteously pissed off. She prided herself on being map smart.

Alyssa stifled a giggle. "I sent you the directions. Where are you lost?"

"Ah, I'm still on Old South Road. State Highway... 45, and...I don't know. I can't find the turnoff."

"What do you mean, you can't find the turnoff? There's a bus stop on the side of the road, and I'm sure there's a sign. Kotahi Bay."

"Are you sure? I haven't seen a sign in ages, and there is no road by a bus stop, not that I've seen."

"Umm..." Alyssa wracked her brain, trying to think back. Had there been a sign? Surely there was. She didn't remember seeing it, now that she came to think of it, but her eyes had been blurry from the tears, and she'd followed her gut back here. Her other home. Her favorite childhood place. "I don't know. Sorry, Kels."

"Look, I want to be there for you, chick, I really do. But I can't spend any more time driving around, getting more and more lost. Are you going to be okay if I head back to town?"

Alyssa slumped to the ground, crossing her legs beneath her. "Yeah, yeah, I'll be okay."

"You don't sound it."

"I'm just...It's a bit lonely. I miss Gran, and I don't have any friends here. It's been too long since I saw you."

"I know. I'm sorry, babe. Look, you'll be back in the city soon, right? We'll catch up then."

"Yeah, I guess. I better go. See ya." Alyssa ended the call before Kelly had a chance to reply. It wasn't her fault that she couldn't find the way to the Bay. Stranger things had happened, and it was getting late.

But, shit. She hadn't realised just how much she'd been looking forward to Kelly arriving. And now she was alone, with a ghost, and June popping up left, right, and centre?

Alyssa's gaze drifted once more to the basement door. She could almost feel the weight of Gran's grimoires calling to her, promising answers, solutions.

No. She wouldn't risk it. Not again. Not ever.

There was only one thing that would brighten her mood now. With just a week until Christmas, it was time to find the tree and decorate it. Gran had a decent sized one even though she'd never been big on Christmas, preferring to celebrate the seasons locally, whatever that meant. Still, when Alyssa was growing up, Gran had heeded her request and ordered an artificial tree from a catalogue; It had always been up when she'd arrived for the summer, waiting for her to decorate.

Alyssa scowled at her painting tools, then dragged them outside to the tap and filled the tray with water. She'd sort it out later. Right now, she had better things to do, and the hallway closet was probably her best bet. It was full of coats and old boxes. The smell of camphor was overwhelming – at least there wouldn't be any moth-riddled clothing here.

And there was a lot of clothing, wasn't there? Old stuff, still in good condition. She pulled it all out, dumping it into piles on the floor, giggling as she did, holding the occasional coat or dress up against her and prancing in front of the hallway mirror. Trying not to think about how this would be a lot more fun with Kelly and a glass of wine.

Each item was in good condition and soon she had a pile of things she could sell on, and a smaller pile of things she intended to keep for herself. Gran had good taste, there was no denying it.

Alyssa had sometimes fancied herself the owner of a little shop. Cool clothing and jewellery. Well, she had all the stock she needed right here to get started. It might not make her big money in the Bay, but she could take it back to the city and they would lap it up there. No doubt about it. The grin plastered on her face was going to keep her awake tonight.

And there was the tree, right at the back, its box tattered, formed more of packing tape than cardboard. She dragged it down the hallway and into the lounge. Paint fumes still lingered, but it wasn't bad enough to put her off and she could leave the windows open until late in this heat.

Alyssa brushed her fingers against the white walls, her fingers coming away dry –perfect painting weather – and then surveyed the room, finally deciding to set the tree up smack bang in the middle, next to the couch, so she didn't have to move it to finish her painting.

Fake trees were never as nice as real ones, but this

would do in a pinch. The branches were old and wilted, but she rammed them into their holes and built it, pyramid like, until it was whole. A sorry excuse for a tree, but nothing that a splash of tinsel and a few decorations couldn't fix.

A breeze drifted past, and she turned to find its origin, sure that she could hear the faint strands of a Christmas carol on it. But then it was gone, like it hadn't been there at all. Alyssa shivered, suddenly feeling a chill, and moved to close all the windows in the room. Her breath fogged in the air, but she turned away, not wanting to acknowledge or see what traces of spirit that might be left on the windows today.

"Must be time for some music and food. I think it's a pizza kind of night," she said to herself, and the ghost. Though, why she was announcing her intentions, she had no idea.

She headed for the kitchen, flicked her phone on to 'shuffle' her music collection, and plugged it into the mini speaker on her keychain. Sound filled the room, making the floor vibrate a little. Alyssa danced around the table as she headed for the fridge, pulling out the pizza bases and toppings she'd got from the store earlier.

With a generous spread of pizza sauce on the base, she added ham and mushrooms, slivers of peppers, and a thick layer of cheese, topping it off with some good old barbeque sauce. She slid it into the preheated oven, pouring herself a glass of crisp white wine.

Alyssa paced the kitchen while she waited for the pizza to cook. She was almost afraid to go back into the living room; there had been a presence, she could sense it, knew that the handprint on the window was only the beginning of what it might do. She didn't mind the chill so much, and as summer got hotter it would definitely save money on cooling the house. And yet...

It might be time to think more seriously about the ritual Gran had told her to do. It hadn't worked the first time but that didn't mean she shouldn't try again. She might not want to become the town witch – she might not want to be any kind of witch – but neither did she particularly want an evil spirit invading her house or hurting anyone. Perhaps she'd missed a step in the ritual the first time, used the wrong herb, or lit the candles in the wrong order.

Alyssa reached for the grimoire, which never seemed to be far from her at the moment, skimming over the page of the ritual, and then the ones before and after, to see if she could figure out where she'd gone wrong. If it hadn't been for Miri, for the fire, she'd know all of this. Maybe then Gran would have been able to tell her more. Prepare her. There was another ritual a few pages later which mentioned the revenant and protection. This had a more complicated setup, which wasn't necessarily a good thing for Alyssa – more ways to screw up – but it was worth a shot.

Surely, being a witch's house, all the ingredients would be here; maybe in the herb drawers June had mentioned, or the secret room below. Alyssa's stomach churned at the thought of venturing down there again. Desire and fear mingling in the worst way. Like two parts of herself that had been separated were attempting to find a way to cohabit inside her body, her mind. The fact that she wanted to use magic at all, to be a conduit for change, for power, twisted her insides. She shouldn't want to do this, but if she didn't get on top of it soon, the chilled temperatures and frosty messages on the window were bound to become something else...something far more serious.

While she wasn't keen to find out, there was a niggle in her chest about this ghost, a feeling that she only had part of the story; her family's side. And her family were assholes. This had been well established. Could she really trust that they had good reasons?

Why had they brought it all the way from the old country? Whatever that meant. Why was it her family's legacy to keep it locked away? Why not banish it to heaven, or hell, or whatever it was witches believed in? The next life, maybe, instead of keeping it in limbo like this?

What irked her most was knowing that Gran hadn't given her any of that information. Not properly. That feeling of disappointment when someone you loved and respected turned out to be not as amazing as you thought chewed at her stomach. She could have spelled it out in the video, made sure that Alyssa had all the information.

And yet...

If it had been enough information for Gran to uphold the legacy, shouldn't it be good enough for her? Except that what Gran did wasn't good enough for her, not according to her mother, anyway. And she'd vowed not to go down that path.

There it was: that lifetime tug between her mother and grandmother. Alyssa loved and respected them both, but had always found it hard to be in between them, and in doing so, was forced to forge her own way, a way that wasn't quite one or the other. And maybe not one that was quite her own either. One where she had a hard time not instantly rejecting things that others tried to force on her.

The oven dinged, drawing Alyssa from that morose line of thought. She pulled the door open, slamming it again when she saw the pizza wasn't quite done. She took another slug of wine and grooved a little to the music, though it couldn't push away the conflict that roiled in her belly.

Looking for a distraction, she dragged the boxes of ornaments to the kitchen table and fished through one, pulling out the tinsel, untangling it from itself. Apparently, the last color scheme Gran had gone for was gold and blue. Alyssa could live with that. For now.

Her fingers tingled when they touched an old box of wooden ornaments. Alyssa remembered these vividly from her childhood: the little drummer boy; the reindeer pulling a sleigh; the angels with their harps and trumpet. So old, so precious. As a child, she would sneak out in the mornings and pull them from the tree, playing games with them along the back of the couch until she heard Gran wake, and then she would rush to return them to their rightful places.

She turned off the oven and rushed to the living room. Her hands moved without thought, placing each on the branch it belonged to, and within minutes, the tree was complete. The last time she'd done this Gran had been in the room and Buttons had been a kitten, skittering around after stray bits of tinsel. The cat was too old for that sort of carry-on now.

Alyssa sat back on her feet. "Perfect. Though I wish you were here to share it with me, Gran." Her nose itched, and she rubbed at it. She wasn't going to cry now though, she had pizza to eat and a ghost to ignore or banish...She still wasn't sure which was the lesser evil.

When she was settled on the couch with dinner and wine, she flicked on the TV again, searching through the channels for something to watch. *Shortland Street* was on, and someone else's drama sounded pretty good right now. She would watch this, eat, and then once the wine had settled her nerves, look for her grandmother's witchy stuff and see about giving that ritual another go. Her gaze went to the last wall left to undercoat, and she knew that tomorrow she'd have to tackle it. She was not spending her Christmas alone in a room with even one yellow wall.

And then she saw it – the carved wooden box – back on the mantle. How many hours ago had it been that she'd moved it to the kitchen? She certainly hadn't brought it back here. She knew it for sure this time. But it had been there when Kelly called, she remembered that now.

Alyssa dumped her plate on the couch and rushed to the front door, opening and closing it, acknowledging the firm click it made as it shut. She would have heard if someone had come in, which meant that the only suspect for the magical moving box was the ghost.

What was it about that particular object? This was the second time it had been moved to the mantle, but Gran hadn't so much as mentioned it in her recorded message.

Not that she'd finished watching. Maybe there was something else on the end of the tape...

Alyssa scrambled back to the couch, hitting play on the VHS player and sitting back to wait, but the only thing left was static. Nothing to explain the box, or the ghost, or anything more. She hit rewind, watched the static roll backward until there was footage again, but when she hit play the only thing visible was what she could only assume was a recent episode of Shortland Street!

Her blood chilled and she drew her legs up from the ground, tucking them beneath her as if the ghost would grab her feet from under the couch.

Something was very off about this. Alyssa could feel it. Surely, Gran wouldn't have left her so unprepared. Not if it was that important to have the ghost contained. There had to have been more on the tape, which meant that someone had tampered with the VHS. Or something.

Alyssa had a feeling there was something dodgy going on, but she wasn't sure what.

Well, at least one mystery had been solved. This box must be the object that bound the ghost.

There were those strange sigils on it, and that thrum of energy she couldn't explain. She wanted the box as far away from her as she could get it, but obviously the ghost was not interested in being removed from the house. She'd watched enough scary movies to know how these things worked. The ghost already had enough power to move the object around, to chill the air and leave impressions on the windows. But that was it so far. No threats, no danger to her aside from the broken glass, which, really, had been her own fault.

Perhaps Gran had been wrong about the ghost?

If only Alyssa knew more, could find out the ghost's name, or some small clue that would help her research the person behind the ghost online. But she only had a mystery, and did she really want to run the risk of the ghost getting stronger? Because it could just be biding its time until it was powerful enough to hurt her. Alyssa chewed on the inside of her bottom lip, the gnawing grasp of uncertainty clawing at her stomach.

Unbidden, the image of the secret room flashed in her mind – shelves lined with ancient tomes, scrolls covered in spidery script. The answers might be down there, waiting. But the thought of delving into that world again, of touching that power...Alyssa's hands shook, phantom heat licking her skin. No. She couldn't. She wouldn't.

Ugh. Her head hurt and it was too late in the day for this kind of thinking. She had a tree, and wine, and no one was getting hurt yet. Surely, another night wouldn't matter.

*You need to decide for yourself...*Gran used to always tell her this. *Stop waiting around for other people to make the decisions for you. You need to be in your power, Alyssa.*

But what if deciding for herself was taking more time to figure things out, not just blindly following instructions?

She moved back to the couch, taking the box with her, running her hands over the intricate carvings before opening the lid.

There was nothing inside since she'd taken the necklace out, which was disappointing. She wasn't sure what she'd expected, but something more than musty air. A name engraved on the inside, a lock of hair. Idly, she considered trying a seance, but she cast the idea aside and sank back on the couch, reaching for her wine as she watched the lights on the tree twinkle in the growing darkness. Before long, her eyelids sagged and she forced herself to head upstairs.

Tonight, she would sleep in Gran's room, because now that she knew the ghost could be anywhere, there was no point getting a sore neck from another night on the couch. She was going to be achy enough from all the painting.

"I just wish there was someone to talk to!" she called out loudly. Not that she wanted a response, but damn it, even a ghost to talk to right now would be better than nothing. "I'm going to bed, by the way. Don't keep me up."

Buttons looked at Alyssa indignantly as she removed him from her lap, but he soon forgave her, dropping to the floor to follow.

She took the box with her just to keep an eye on it. She'd clean up in the morning and to hell with those memories of Gran telling her that the job is much easier if you tidy when the mess is made. Grief had taken a backseat right now, and all she could feel was irritation that the woman had just dumped a ghost on her lap and thought she was going to willingly deal with it, like an obedient little girl.

As she climbed the stairs, Alyssa's gaze drifted to the basement door once more. The secret room called to her. Her fingers trembled on the banister. No. She wouldn't go down that path again. She couldn't. Not tonight. She wasn't ready.

No wonder Alyssa's mother had cut ties with Gran. All witchiness aside, it was a major burden to have unwanted expectations dumped on your shoulders. Alyssa didn't like it at all.

That night, her dreams were restless, filled with flickering shadows and whispered incantations. In them, she stood at the top of the basement stairs, staring down into inky darkness. Something moved in the gloom, beckoning. The scent of old leather and sage wafted up, mingling with the metallic tang of blood. She took a step forward, drawn by an inexorable pull. But then fire erupted around her. Alyssa woke with a strangled gasp, sheets tangled around her legs, sweat cooling on her brow.

She lay there, heart thundering in her chest, as the first grey light of dawn crept through the curtains. The box sat on the nightstand, its carvings throwing strange shadows in the dim light. Alyssa turned away from it, burying her face in the pillow. She couldn't keep ignoring this. She had to do something. Soon.

Even as she thought it, a chill breeze caressed her cheek, carrying the faint scent of lavender – Gran's favourite perfume. Alyssa squeezed her eyes shut, willing the morning to come faster, to chase away the shadows of the night and the ghosts that lurked within them.

11

ALYSSA

Alyssa woke in the night to a thump from the kitchen beneath her. Actually, it sounded a little like a chair being dragged across the wooden floor. A weird scraping that sent shivers down her spine.

Damn. She should have done that spell. She should have sucked it up and just bloody well done it.

She contemplated dragging the covers over her head and ignoring the sound, but it was louder now, moving from the kitchen down the hall towards the lounge. The slow drag of something hard against the floor. Oh shit. Next there would be rattling chains and mournful wailing to go along with it.

No, dammit. This was her house now, and she wasn't going to let a ghost take over – even if it had been her negligence that had allowed it to happen. This was so typical of her; ignore the problem and hope it went away, only for it to explode in her face.

She got out of bed and shoved her feet into slippers. There was no chill in the air, not like the last few times. She wished for a baseball bat or something, though what good that would do against a spirit...

"I can hear you!" Alyssa shouted, slamming open the door of the bedroom. "I'm not afraid, do you hear me? I'm not scared of you!"

As she charged down the stairs, there was an almighty crash from the lounge and she rounded the corner to see her tree, toppled over, a massacre of tinsel and ornaments strewn across the room, and the windows cast wide, letting a cool night breeze flow through.

"You asshole! Bloody ghost!" Alyssa balled her fists up, wanting something to punch. Instead, she crossed the lounge and slammed the windows shut, pulling the curtains closed and turning to survey the damage.

There was a chirp, and a flash of feathers, and Alyssa spotted a pīwakawaka flitting around the room, the flash of its tail fan swishing through the air.

Alyssa froze. She knew the lore; that a fantail *inside* the house was thought to be a tohu, often it was an omen of death...but someone had already died.

She flung the window open again, hoping the bird

would see itself out. Tears pricked her eyes as she dropped to her knees and drew the little wooden drummer boy from the wreckage. One of his drumsticks was gone, splintered at his hand. Fat tears dripped down her cheeks, tumbling down her chest as she clutched the old figurine tight.

"I'm sorry, Gran. I never meant for this to happen. I should have listened." A sob lurched out of her throat and she dropped the ornament, flinging herself on the couch. She lay there for a few minutes, eyes scanning the wreckage, heart aching from the loss, until she noticed the chill filling the room. "What the hell do you want now? Haven't you done enough for one night?"

The chill turned arctic, and she drew the couch blanket around her. It still smelled like Gran; the scent comforted her but didn't stave off the fear. A memory surfaced – Gran teaching her a simple protection charm, showing her how to weave energy into a shield. Alyssa's fingers twitched, muscle memory urging her to trace the patterns in the air. But she clenched her fists, pushing the instinct away.

The icy air moved like fingers up her leg, her arm, through her hair, almost like it was...comforting her? What the hell? She sat upright, shrugging as if it would dislodge the spirit fingers.

"I don't know what the hell you think you're doing, but I'm going to destroy you. Do you know that?"

She heard another scrape then, like fingers on glass, and she rushed to the window, pulling the curtains aside to see what message the ghost had left for her now. Streetlight shone through the pane, making the words very clear.

It was not me.

"What do you mean, it wasn't you? Who the hell else could it be?" Alyssa waited, but there were no further sounds, no more messages appearing on the window. She reached out, her fingers trailing against the chilly glass, erasing the ghost's words.

Her hands shook as she withdrew them, the cold from the window seeping through her skin. They hadn't been that cold when she'd shut them before. So perhaps the ghost wasn't lying, maybe there was someone playing tricks on her to get her to think she was being haunted.

But to what end? She wasn't going to run – but perhaps the haunter didn't know that. Maybe they were relying on her being a scared little girl who wasn't invested enough in the property to stick around. If things got too hard, she would just leave, right? There was nothing tying her to this place. No friends. No job. No family, now.

Alyssa's mind raced. If not the ghost, then who?

Mrs Nolan, attempting to scare her into taking up her grandmother's role? June's face flashed before her, that hungry look in her eyes when she'd asked about the carved box. Even Derek and his weird questions. Samantha's words echoed in her ears – warnings about those who might seek to use the power in this house for their own ends; perhaps she had an ulterior motive too. A chill that had nothing to do with spirits ran down her spine.

She scraped the tinsel from the floor, carrying an armful through the kitchen and out the back door to the bin, along with the trashed Christmas tree. Once she'd picked the bits off her PJs, she turned to survey the backyard. Moonlight spilled down through the tree branches, revealing Buttons in the grass.

"Hey, boy, come here. What are you doing outside, you old fool? I thought you were still in bed." The cat didn't budge and her stomach turned. "Buttons?"

She moved slowly, hoping that he'd get up, or meow. Anything. But by the time she was a few feet away, she realised that what she was actually seeing was a grave marker and a carved stone cat. She knelt beside it and reached out to stroke the cool stone, reading the engraving on the grave marker: Buttons....departed this world in June last year?

He was dead. Had been dead this whole time... And yet...

Alyssa glanced back at the house, could make out the shape of Buttons standing in the open doorway.

He'd been her main companion since she'd arrived in the Bay.

She looked back at the tombstone and the letters of June seemed to glow, sending a shiver down her spine. Was that meant to be a message? The ghost telling her who was behind the haunting? She shuddered, thinking about how often the woman was in her house, about her saccharine approach. Surely it couldn't be her?

"Buttons?" she called, turning back to the door, and the cat leapt down the step and headed towards her, butting his head against her leg. Cold, but there. Solid enough, yet...gone.

Apparently, Gran had left her not one, but two ghosts. Alyssa shook her head, a twisted laugh escaping her lips.

And now she was thinking about it, more things were clicking into place; June's desire for the box – the one connected to the ghost, her 'helpful' comments. The way Buttons always left the house when June entered.

She froze, thinking back to how Mrs Nolan had tossed all the muffins away, saying that they were bad. Had June been trying to poison her or something? Alyssa's hand went to her mouth, her stomach roiling, recalling how awful she'd felt the morning after she'd had some of the chamomile tea.

Bloody June. It had to be her. That woman was there every day, being mortified at the changes, swearing that Sylvie would roll over in her grave if she could see what Alyssa was doing to the place. It seemed like she not only wanted Gran's ghost, but her house as well.

Alyssa would never let her have either, not now. Not ever. It was time to fight 'ghost' with ghost.

With trembling hands, she reached for that spark inside her, that well of energy she'd kept locked away for so long. It responded eagerly, warming her from the inside out. She stood, determination hardening her features. Whoever was behind this would rue the day they decided to mess with *this witch.*

12

BUTTONS

Mreeeowwww

13

ALYSSA

After a little digging, Alyssa found all the required items for keeping the ghost contained. She didn't know exactly what she was doing, but she had a feeling that if she botched the ritual badly enough, whatever protections were still left on the house would be torn apart – and then she could make a bargain with the spirit. Whatever reason there had been for keeping it locked up, she would use it to drive June away. After the ghost's assurances that it wasn't the one who caused the damage, she could only think that it was the lesser evil.

And right now, she needed to follow her intuition. To trust herself. Gran had always told her that, even in their very last phone call just a week before she'd died. “Trust yourself, dear one, you have everything you need right inside you.”

As Alyssa gathered the components and took them into the living room, her hands trembled. Old memories flared up and threatened to overwhelm her. But beneath the fear, she felt something else stirring – a thrum of energy, an awakening power that both terrified and exhilarated her.

"I can do this," she whispered, clenching her fists. "I have to do this."

She had nothing to lose, not really. Gran was dead, so was Buttons – and the ghost, come to think of it – and if Alyssa really had to leave the house, she would. She'd had no time to put down roots, and maybe it was better that way. The idea of having her own home was appealing, but she'd lived without it for years now and she could carry on like that if necessary. Better for it all to explode now than for her to get settled and then have it happen.

Exploding things was something she was good at. Picking up the pieces after? While less fun, she’d had plenty of practice.

Alyssa chugged back a preparatory glass of wine – she needed all the fortification she could get – and took a deep breath.

She closed her eyes, reaching for that spark inside her, that well of power she'd kept locked away for so long. It responded eagerly, warming her from the inside out. This time, instead of shying away, she embraced it, letting it fill her.

First, she laid out a circle of salt, and then she kicked holes in it. She laid the corners out in the wrong places and then burned everything required for the ritual in the middle in one go. The stench was so bad that she had to swing open the windows and pray that none of the neighbours called the fire department. She could have been burning corpses from the smell of it.

As the acrid smoke filled the air, Alyssa felt a surge of...something. Power? Recognition? The scent seemed to awaken something primal within her, a knowledge buried deep in her bones. Her fingers tingled and she found herself tracing symbols in the air without conscious thought.

"Come on! If this doesn't work to set you free, I don't know what will. But just know it was me, okay? I did this!" She willed the ghost to understand her desire, to be gentle on her, to understand that she wasn't trying to trick it or treat it badly.

Nothing stirred for a moment, and then an icy breeze shot through the lounge, forcing the smoke out through the window and cleansing the house of the stench. Alyssa relaxed a little once she could see properly again, though no ghosts were present.

"Well, I guess it worked. Can you give me some sign that you're here?"

Instantly, the temperature dropped about twenty degrees. Alyssa shuddered, totally unprepared for that level of cold. She reached for the couch blanket, drawing it around her again; the last piece of comfort she had available. "That answers that question..."

The temperature continued to drop until she could feel the moisture wick out of her skin, each breath fogged in front of her. She could hear the breath of another, and her heart quickened as icy fingers traced her cheek. She closed her eyes, jaw clenched, waiting for the ghost to lash out.

Droplets of moisture fell on her face and she opened her eyes.

It was snowing.

Inside her house.

Alyssa's jaw dropped, and her tongue darted out, catching a flake. Her hands came up, fingers spread wide, and she spun, just like a girl in a movie. "Oh. My. God. It's snowing."

As the flakes swirled around her, Alyssa felt a rush of pure joy. This was magic – real, tangible, beautiful magic. And she had made it happen. The realisation hit her like a bolt of lightning. She wasn't just a bystander in this supernatural world; she was an active participant. A creator.

"You're welcome."

Alyssa froze at the masculine voice that invaded the living room. She turned, and there, by the tree, was a ghost looking entirely unlike any ghost she'd expected to show up. For starters, he appeared solid – none of this wispy, ghoulish shit – and second, he was surprisingly good looking. He wore a deep blue woollen tunic over brown linen trousers, complete with fur-lined boots, and a cloak. His long hair was braided back from his face and a thick beard dangled to mid-chest. As a whole, it was a very good look on him.

Obviously, it had been too long since she'd been in the company of men if she was thinking about a ghost that way. Way too long.

"So, you're the powerful, scary ghost that's been knocking around my house?" Alyssa put her hands on her hips to still their trembling and tried to look in control.

The ghost tilted his head to one side and stared at her. "Not knocking about. Just...testing my limits." He gave her a mocking grin and shrugged nonchalantly. She noticed the axe that hung at his side and tried not to shudder.

"But you didn't knock over my tree to scare me away?" She raised an eyebrow, attempting to maintain the facade that she wasn't petrified right now. A tiny part of her brain was screaming though, and the rest of it was arguing that he hadn't killed her just yet, so, maybe this would all be okay.

"No, but we both know who did." He stood there so calm, so passive, nothing like the raging spirit she'd expected. Gran had said he was evil, a rampaging revenant and all that. Was he trying to lull her into a false sense of security? Or was this some ploy to trick her?

"Yeah, I got your messages," she said. "Why warn me though? I don't understand. You're meant to hate my family, and yet..." She bit her lip, suddenly uncertain, feeling like that she'd swum into a riptide without noticing.

"And yet I haven't harmed you?" He raised an eyebrow, something sardonic about his face.

"Well. Yeah." Her shoulders slumped. This was not at all the confrontation she'd been expecting. But then...what had she expected? Nothing, exactly, because she'd unbound the protection spell on a whim and an intuition.

"What do you want?" she asked, knowing there had to be a catch.

"Your first-born child?" He raised an eyebrow and gave her a wry smile.

It was a punch to the guts. Her long-term boyfriend had dumped her a few months ago after they'd received the crushing news that she was infertile. Not just a low probability of fertility, but genetically unable to have children. The news had anchored in Alyssa's deep fear of being somehow wrong, not enough, defective. But now? Now she was taking her power back, infertility be damned.

"Unfortunately for you, I'm infertile, so there won't be any children from me." The bitter words spilled out, but he seemed unfazed.

"All I want is my freedom. The women of your line have kept me trapped for hundreds of years because your ancestor couldn't have what she wanted."

"What did she want?" Alyssa asked, her curiosity outweighing the fear and confusion she felt.

The ghost drifted across the room until they were inches apart. "Me." His word pushed frigid air past her face and she shivered.

It took a moment to sink in. "You mean my ancestors have been keeping you locked up for hundreds of years because you wouldn't..." She couldn't finish the sentence. It was so petty, so ridiculous. She couldn't believe anyone would do that, let alone that her relations back through the ages would be complicit in this. Though, perhaps that explained why her family was mostly a pack of jerks. "Was she ugly?"

The ghost laughed. The sound echoed around the frosty room, causing the snow to stop. It began to melt, the individual flakes turning to liquid and dripping down her skin. God, that was going to be horrible for the carpet and the paint; her new paint! At least she'd only done the undercoat.

"Is that a yes?"

"No, she was not ugly, not on the outside, anyway. I just wasn't interested. Surely you know well enough that not all men will slip into bed with a beautiful woman."

"But she was a witch! And she...God, did she kill you?" Alyssa frowned, incredulous. If this was her legacy, she didn't want any part of it. How had Gran thought this was a good idea?

"It wasn't quite as straightforward as that."

Alyssa felt some of the tension leave her body, but not all. "So, she didn't kill you?"

"She killed my body, captured my spirit." The ghost watched her, as though assessing her response.

What good response could there be? Her frown deepened and she shook her head, not wanting to believe it. The ghost could be making this up, trying to make her feel sorry for him, but it seemed too preposterous to be a lie.

"When you put it that way, it sounds even worse than killing you. But then, you're not dead, so...No, I don't know. Do you think it's worse? My head hurts. I need a glass of wine." Alyssa sat down on the couch and reached for her glass; it was even colder with snow having landed in it.

"You drink a lot of wine."

"Oh great, you're giving me grief about the amount of wine I drink? No wonder Gran told me to keep you locked up. You've been free for five minutes and you're already making my life more difficult!" Alyssa buried her face in her hands.

"Would you prefer I smash something? I could slam some doors, or, I don't know, what would you like?"

Alyssa lifted her face and considered the ghost for a moment, remembering the whole reason she had released it. "I want to get June out of this house permanently. I want her to never set foot on the property again. In fact, it would be better if she left town completely."

"So that vengeful trait runs in the family, after all." He quirked an eyebrow.

Alyssa glared at him. "If you help me, I will do everything I can to break this binding for you. Whatever it takes to set you completely free from the curse placed on you. It's not just for me, you know. June wants you. I don't know what she knows, or what she intends to do with you, but she wants you, and she's been trying to scare me off. Who knows what else she's capable of? Do you really want a woman like that having control over you?"

His jaw clenched, and he moved away from her, floating across the room and fading from sight before coming back stronger than before.

"No. I think we can work together, but I need you to swear to me that you will fulfill your end of the bargain once this woman is suitably dealt with."

"I will, I promise."

He laughed again, but this time there was no humour in it. "Your line has made me promises in the past. You're not the first to set me loose, only to box me up again when my usefulness passed. I require a blood oath."

She flung her hands into the air, frustrated and trying not to be frightened. "What do you think I am? I don't know how to do that!"

"You're a witch, just like the rest of them." His lip curled. "I can smell it on you."

Alyssa felt a flare of indignation, but beneath it, a spark of...pride? "Maybe I am," she said, straightening her spine. "Maybe it's time I stopped running from that. But don't think I'm like them. I'm my own person."

She closed her eyes, reaching deep within herself, tapping into that well of power she'd kept locked away for so long. When she opened them again, they seemed to glow with an inner light. "Tell me what to do."

The ghost regarded her with newfound respect. "Very well. Take your grandmother's athame. Cut your palm and let seven drops of blood fall into the binding circle."

She quickly created a fresh circle, this time leaving it intact. Alyssa's hands shook as she retrieved the ritual knife, its blade gleaming in the moonlight. For a moment, she hesitated, the memory of fire and pain threatening to overwhelm her. But then she thought of Buttons, of June's smug face, of all the secrets and lies that had shaped her life.

"No more running," she whispered, and drew the blade across her palm.

As her blood fell, she felt a surge of power unlike anything she'd ever experienced. The room seemed to pulse with energy, and she could feel the threads of magic weaving around her, binding her to her promise.

"I, Alyssa Whenua, swear on my blood and my power to free you once June has been dealt with. So shall it be."

The words came unbidden, as if spoken by some deeper part of herself. As the last syllable fell from her lips, she felt something fundamental shift within her. She was no longer just Alyssa, the girl who ran from her heritage. She was Alyssa *the witch*, embracing her birthright at last.

"Excellent. It seems that we have a deal then." The ghost drifted near the window, his form flickering like northern lights.

"What was it like?" Alyssa said, softly. "When you were alive...if you don't mind me asking?"

"I can still smell the pine smoke from our long-house, hear the drums beating under northern stars as we worked our magic. The fjords were our temples – every stone and tree held power for those who knew how to listen." His form shimmered, and for a moment Alyssa caught the scent of woodsmoke and sea salt, felt the bite of arctic wind.

I was völva," he said suddenly, his voice distant with memory. "A seer, a worker of seiðr magic."

"Like a Viking witch?" Alyssa asked, intrigued despite her lingering wariness.

"Something like that." A wry smile touched his lips. "I had the sight from childhood – dreams that came true, visions in the flames. My mother taught me in secret, passed down her knowledge of the old ways. We would paint the runes in blood and honey, weave spells into the threads of our garments. My mother's fingers were always stained with juniper and yarrow, her hair bound with tokens of bone and amber." His voice held a distant longing. "The magic was different then – wild and close to the earth, bound to our survival, like the cry of ravens or the crackle of ice over deep water."

He turned to face her, and for a moment Alyssa saw him as he must have been in life – proud and fierce, marked with runes of power. "After I came of age, I began traveling between villages, reading omens, healing the sick, helping souls pass peacefully to the next world. I was powerful – renowned. Until I met her. Your ancestor."

"What was her name?" Alyssa asked.

"Astrid." His form flickered again, agitated. "She had come from Norway, seeking power in the new world. When she saw what I could do...she wanted me to teach her everything I knew. But seiðr cannot be learned so quickly. It requires patience, respect for the old ways. She wouldn't listen."

“What happened?”

"When I refused to share my secrets, she..." He faltered. "The spell she used was dark magic, forbidden. It trapped not just my body but my very soul, binding me to that box. She thought she could force me to teach her, but even death would have been better than that betrayal of my craft."

The raw pain in his voice made Alyssa's chest ache. She understood now why he had chosen to trust her – she had offered him freedom without demanding anything in return. Had seen him as a person, not just a source of power.

"I'm sorry," she said quietly. "For what my family did to you."

The ghost inclined his head, a gesture of acknowledgment. "You are not her," he said. "I've watched your line for centuries. Some were kind, some cruel. But you...you remind me of my mother. She understood that true power comes from respect, not control."

The comparison warmed something in Alyssa's chest.

“Now, I’ll leave you.” He gave her a curt nod and then vanished, taking the chill from the room as he went.

Alyssa felt suddenly at a loss. She dragged her fingers across the carpet, but not a drop of moisture remained to suggest that it had been snowing. In her living room.

She'd never seen it snow before, and she kind of wished the ghost would make it happen again. After all, it was almost Christmas, and this might be her only chance for a white one.

Hell, she'd just let a ghost loose from hundreds of years of capture, was set on avenging her dead grandmother’s dead cat, and here she was wishing for snow.

Kelly would smack her over the head if she were here. But of course, she wasn't.

Alyssa poured herself another glass of wine, but this time, it wasn't to drown her sorrows or numb her fear. It was a toast – to new beginnings, to embracing her power, to facing whatever came next head-on.

As she sipped, she felt the magic humming beneath her skin, a constant reminder of the path she'd chosen. There would be no going back now. But for the first time since arriving in Kotahi Bay, Alyssa felt truly alive.

Alyssa left the mess from the unbinding on the floor and headed to bed, dreams of power and possibility swirling through her mind.

When she got to her room though, she dragged Gran's journal out and sat with it on the bed. While the ghost's story had the ring of truth about it, she wanted to see if she could find some other clues about what had really happened. Whether her grandmother had known the true story; whatever that turned out to be.

The journal's pages were filled with Gran's flowing script, but these weren't just spell recipes. They were whakapapa – the genealogy of their family's connection to the land, over time, stories of how their ancestors first learned to connect with the earth's power.

Our gift comes with responsibility, Gran had written. *We are kaitiaki – guardians. The earth mother gives us strength, but in return we must protect and nurture her children. The trees, the birds, the stones, the waters – all are sacred. All are connected.*

Alyssa's fingers trembled as she turned the pages. Here was the truth of her heritage – not just in spells and symbols, but in this profound connection to the land itself. Her power wasn't something to fear; it was a gift from Papatūānuku, meant to heal and protect.

The incident that had scarred Miri – she understood it differently now. She'd been trying to force the power then, to bend it to her will instead of working in harmony with it. No wonder it had backfired so dramatically.

And it seemed like her ancestors had been trying to do the same thing with the ghost. Forcing him, bending his will. The thought twisted her stomach into a pretzel.

If that was the truth of it, then she was compelled to do something to rectify it.

14

ALYSSA

A chill woke her in the morning, a sharp contrast to the muggy heat of the night, which had made her toss and turn. Alyssa's skin prickled, goosebumps rising along her arms. She blinked blearily, the room coming into focus. Perhaps she could convince the spirit to sit by her bedside all night and keep her cool.

The thought startled her. Just days ago, she'd been terrified of the supernatural. Now here she was, considering a ghost as a potential air conditioner. How quickly things changed.

Yeah, she was really losing it now. She wished Buttons was here, so that she had someone to talk to, someone who wouldn't think she was totally insane. But then, if she was talking to a ghost cat, perhaps she was. Maybe she'd even imagined the visitation from last night. Yet the chill put paid to that daydream.

Alyssa sat up, running a hand through her tangled hair. The room felt different somehow, charged with an energy she couldn't quite name. She could almost taste it on her tongue, metallic and wild.

And hers.

"So, how are we going to do this?" The ghost's voice made her sit upright, pulling the covers around her. He had a European accent of some sort, and yet he spoke English with ease.

His sudden appearance sent her heart racing, a mix of fear and exhilaration coursing through her veins. She was really doing this. Consorting with spirits, delving into magic. There was no going back now.

"Where did you come from?"

"I was downstairs." He hovered in the doorway, almost looking like a regular man casually leaning against the frame.

Alyssa rolled her eyes. "I meant, you know, in history, what country?"

"I was a Viking once, though it has been many years since I was home." A pained expression flared across his features before they smoothed out again.

Images flashed through Alyssa's mind – longships cutting through icy waters, fierce warriors with braided beards. The ghost before her suddenly seemed ancient, a relic of a time long past. It made her feel small, yet strangely significant. Here she was, bridging centuries.

"And you speak English, like me."

"When you have nothing to do but sit around and rail against your bindings for hundreds of years, you pick up a thing or two." He gave a little shrug.

"And your name?"

He shook his head. "I'll not give you that, not yet."

Alyssa felt a flare of frustration, tinged with wariness. Names had power, she knew that much from her grandmother's teachings. His reluctance was telling.

"Well, that's going to make this pretty awkward then." Alyssa shoved the blankets off, glad she was the pajama wearing type, and grabbed her robe from the chair. The soft fabric against her skin was comforting, a small bit of normalcy in this surreal situation. "So what should I call you then? Mr Ghost? Viking man?"

"Mr Ghost has a nice ring to it." His words were filled with amusement.

"Nice to meet you, Mr Ghost. My name is Alyssa."

"I have known you since you were a child, Alyssa. Even when I was powerless to act, I have been able to watch." He watched her now too, his gaze firm.

A shiver ran down Alyssa's spine. The idea of being watched her whole life, unknowing, was unsettling. Yet there was also a strange comfort in it, like she'd had a silent guardian all along.

"Your grandmother had meant to train you to take on her role, but that didn't really work out, did it?" He cocked an eyebrow.

Alyssa let out a rough laugh as she moved towards the doorway. "No, Mum wasn't too thrilled when she found out. And after what happened with Miri..." Alyssa looked away from the ghost, a chill freezing her body, but this time it wasn't because of the spectre in her room.

The ghost would have seen what happened. Would know what she had done...

"She was not the worst, your grandmother," he said, almost as though he was changing the subject or could feel her tension. "She meant no harm to me, or you, or anyone."

"So," Alyssa said, tugging on her earlobe as she started towards the stairs. "If you could watch, you have all the gossip about June."

She headed for the kitchen, unsurprised to find that the ghost had skipped ahead of her and appeared to be sitting at the table. The kitchen felt different with him there, smaller somehow. The air seemed to thicken, heavy with unspoken secrets. Alyssa's fingers trembled slightly as she filled the jug and prepared her coffee while it boiled, but the familiar routine grounded her, had her pondering the ease with which she was adapting to this situation. Witchiness in the blood-line, feuds in the family, ghosts in the house. Yeah, all just a part of life...

"There is more to the woman than you might think, and unlike your grandmother, she is not one of the good ones. She lusts after power, and it was for that reason she seduced Sylvie."

Alyssa snorted coffee out of her nose as she spun around. "She what? My grandmother was having sex with that woman?" She fell into a chair at the table, shaking her head in disbelief. "I just...I don't...I can't get my head around the idea. Wow."

The revelation hit her like a physical blow. Her grandmother, who she'd always seen as this paragon of virtue and chastity, suddenly seemed more human, more fallible. It was both disappointing and strangely comforting. How had she never thought about the fact that Gran had always been alone? Alyssa had never even heard a mention of a husband, father, or grandfather; which was very strange, now that she thought about it.

"She was lonely, and June gave the appearance of caring for her. They bonded over their magic, and while Sylvie's was stronger, June was manipulative. When she finally revealed her true nature, your grandmother ended things and banished June from the house."

Alyssa fought back a wave of doubt. How easily she'd fallen into trusting this ghost's version of events!

Wasn't that exactly what June had done to Gran – appeared caring and trustworthy before revealing her true nature? For all she knew, he could be manipulating her just as skillfully, playing on her sympathy and rage to achieve his own ends.

She'd freed him from centuries of imprisonment without really questioning why her ancestors had thought it necessary to keep him bound.

The ghost's story about her ancestor's spurned advances seemed almost too neat, too sympathetic.

And yet...there was something in the way he spoke about Gran, a genuine respect in his voice. He could have hurt her at any point since being freed, could have taken violent revenge for his long imprisonment.

Instead, he'd been helping her, warning her about June.

Still, she'd have to stay alert, watch for any sign that this alliance wasn't what it seemed. She wouldn't let herself be as blind to betrayal as Gran had been.

Alyssa's mind raced, piecing together fragments of memories. That photo on the mantle, June's familiarity with the house, her sense of entitlement. It all made a sickening sort of sense now.

"Did they live together?" Alyssa asked, suddenly wishing she had known. Wishing that Gran had felt able to tell her about this part of her life.

"Not entirely. Though they spent most of their time here, June always maintained her own house. It doesn't bear thinking to consider what she might do there."

"It's really hard to get my head around this."

"Skills in baking make one less likely to be evil natured?" The ghost quirked his eyebrow. “Besides, you have no idea what she was putting into those muffins.”

Alyssa’s blood ran cold as she recalled the way Mrs Nolan had thrown that first batch in the bin. And the tea!

"No, I didn't mean it like that, it's just...Well, she all but had me fooled, too. And to think I was on the verge of giving her what she wanted.” She was such a fool. So easy to manipulate. A doormat, Grant would probably say. A pang of sorrow hit her in the gut as she thought of her grandmother in those last months. Alone, again. “Do you think she ever really loved Gran? I hope so, or at least, I hope Gran believed it. She deserved to be loved." Alyssa shut up and sipped her coffee until it was done, trying to still the flock of thoughts swooping through her brain. None of them were really helping right now, and she had to get her facts straight.

The bitter taste of the coffee grounded her, cutting through the swirl of emotions. She focused on the warmth of the mug in her hands, the solid presence of the table beneath her elbows. Real, tangible things in a world that suddenly seemed anything but.

Thankfully, the ghost was blessedly quiet.

"Right. So, June is a powerful witch. And a bitch. She tried to use my grandmother. She knows about you, and she wants your box. Is there anything else she wants?"

"The house itself is a vessel." The ghost gestured to the kitchen walls, the ceiling. "They have performed years of magic beneath this roof. It imbeds itself in a place. June is newer to town than your grandmother was, and much of her magic was done here too. It would make sense that she wants the house as a power base."

Alyssa frowned, not liking what the ghost had to say about things. There was still something she didn't quite understand though. "But what does she want with you? You're just a ghost, right?"

His lips twitched into a smile. "Not 'just' a ghost, not really. I may no longer walk the earth, but I have a power of my own –why do you think your ancestors have kept me locked up? For fear that I might take my vengeance against your line. Rightful vengeance."

The air shimmered between them, crystalising into frost. For the first time since she had set him free, Alyssa knew fear. She swallowed hard, the chill burning her nostrils, her throat. The temperature in the room plummeted, and she could see her breath misting in the air. Her heart pounded, a primal part of her recognising the predator before her.

"But you will not cross me, will you, Alyssa? We have made a deal."

"A deal. Yes. And today we'll seal it in blood." She nodded, reached for her earlobe and tugged it so hard she flinched.

"Now."

"Um, you want to do it right now? I'm not even properly dressed."

"I've seen you in less."

Her cheeks flushed, and she tensed up. Goddammit, this ghost was catching her off guard way too often.

"All the same, I'd rather get dressed before I go making incisions and leaking blood everywhere. Why don't you do your ghostly magic and get whatever is needed ready in the lounge, and I'll be there soon." She gave him a pointed look, resisted the urge to poke out her tongue, and headed for the bedroom.

As she dressed, Alyssa's mind whirled. She was about to make a second pact with a centuries-old Viking ghost. The absurdity of it all threatened to overwhelm her. Yet beneath the fear and doubt, there was a growing sense of...rightness. Like she was finally stepping into a role she'd been meant to play all along.

Alyssa dragged her fingers through her limp hair, then pulled on yesterday's clothes. She would shower after this was done, though how she was going to guarantee that Mr Pervy wasn't watching, she had no idea.

It didn't matter. She felt sick to her stomach knowing that Gran had been used – not just by June, but by her ancestors as well. What kind of stock were they from that a woman felt she was entitled to rip the life from a man and keep him captive across time, simply for denying her?

Regardless of June's designs on the ghost and the house, Alyssa would have let the ghost free after hearing the truth and feeling the way that it resonated in her chest. There was truth in his words, earth deep. She only hoped that Gran hadn't known the full story, because surely, if she had, she would have done the same as Alyssa intended.

"Right, better get this over with," she muttered to herself.

When she entered the lounge, the air felt thick, charged with potential. The candles were set in their proper places, and the circle of salt was perfect. The ghost was seated on the floor in the middle and beckoned to her. Alyssa's heart raced, her palms suddenly slick with sweat. This was it. No turning back now.

"You're way better at this than I am," she commented, stepping into the circle and sitting across from him. A knife lay to one side, its sharp edge glinting in the flickering candlelight.

"I have more practice, that is all. Under other circumstances, you could have been a great witch, but I get the feeling it is not really your thing."

"You're pretty perceptive for a dead guy." Alyssa smiled at him, despite the seriousness of their setting. "Let's get this over with. What do we do?"

"Take the knife, slice your thumb across the pad, and let the blood drop into the bowl."

She peered into it, but all she could make out was a dark liquid. "Do I want to know what's in there?"

"Probably not." He gave a slight shake of his head, his lips twitching in amusement. He gestured for her to pick up the knife and closed his eyes. So trusting. Though, it wasn't like she could stab him or anything. A low hum emanated from his throat.

She recognised the blade from the night before. It was cool in her hands, heavier than it looked. For a moment she thought about lying – it's not like he could see – but then she pushed that thought away and cut into her skin, the edge of the blade piercing her easily. She let out a gasp at the pain – always the minor cuts that hurt the most – and dropped the knife so she could squeeze her blood into the bowl below. It wasn't much, but she had done as he'd asked.

The scent of copper filled the air, mingling with the smoke from the candles. Alyssa felt lightheaded, whether from the blood loss or the gravity of what she was doing, she couldn't tell.

The ghost opened his eyes and looked into the bowl. The liquid mixed itself; more of his fancy ghost antics, she guessed.

"Do you, Alyssa, on your word and life agree to free me of all my bonds and ties in exchange for removing June from your life?"

"You're not going to kill her, are you?"

"No."

"Then yes. I agree to free you once our deal is complete."

"Drink it."

"What, now? I don't know about that."

He laughed. "Drink it, and then I'll tell you my name."

Alyssa pursed her lips. She was going to have to drink it anyway, otherwise the ghost wouldn't help her, and who knew what hell he'd wreak if she didn't. At least he was going to give her something for her trouble.

She grabbed the bowl with both hands and lifted it to her mouth, letting the thick, foul tasting liquid slip down her throat. It burned, tasting of copper and something ancient, unknowable. She fought the urge to gag, forcing herself to swallow every drop.

"Oh god, that was gross." She wiped at her lips, trying to eradicate the taste. "I'm really glad you didn't tell me what was in that."

"My name is Magnus."

Alyssa blinked at him, surprised at the admission. Trying desperately not to think too hard about what she'd just consumed.

"Well, I wouldn't have picked you for a Magnus, but I guess it's not too bad." The tang in her throat was fading, and she felt a little woozy. Maybe she should have made him tell her what was in that drink after all. "Are we done here? I think I want to go get cleaned up, and then..."

"Lie down," he said gently.

"You read my mind."

"I know what you've consumed."

"You didn't poison me, did you? I'd be really unhappy about that." The room was spinning now. Alyssa blinked, her eyelids getting heavier each time they closed. Panic fluttered in her chest, but it felt distant, muffled. She tried to stand, but her legs wouldn't cooperate. She was tilting over, her head hitting – a pillow? When had that gotten there?

She forced her eyes open once more and felt a gust of wind as the ghost blew the candles out.

"I didn't poison you. Just rest." He brushed back the strands of her hair from her face and gazed down at her, but her vision blurred and then it was black.

As consciousness slipped away, Alyssa couldn't shake the feeling that she'd just set something monumental in motion. For better or worse, her life would never be the same. The last thing she heard before succumbing to darkness was Magnus's voice, low and ancient:

"Sleep now, little witch. When you wake, your true journey begins."

15

MAGNUS

The witch slept more deeply than he had expected her to; but then, he had to give her some grace. It had been a long week for her, and she had learned more secrets about her family in that short time than in the whole rest of her life.

He'd seen her as a child, at the knee of Sylvie, learning small magics, exploring her abilities, but the woman she had become was so different. Scared of her power, leaving things to the fates rather than claiming her own destiny. And yet, she had brokered the deal. She was attempting to free him and right the wrongs of the past, which was more than anyone from her line had done before.

That took a certain bravery.

A certain rage.

The kind of rage that matched his own, which was tempered now by this woman. He could tell that she had heard the truth in his words; had felt things snap into place.

Sweat beaded on her forehead as she slept, as the concoction worked its way through her body, and Magnus snapped his fingers, chilling the air for her and brushing his cool, ghostly fingers across her brow.

16

ALYSSA

Sunlight streamed through the window and probed the back of her eyes. Alyssa raised a hand to cover them before sitting up. The light seemed to dance and shimmer, charged with an energy that hadn't been there before. Alyssa blinked, wondering if it was a side effect of the ritual or if her perception had somehow been altered.

The room was still a mess, though it didn't look as bad as she thought it should. Candle wax had dripped onto the floor, forming strange, rune-like patterns. The salt circle remained unbroken, a testament to the power of the ritual they'd performed. And there was a thumping at the door, which was probably what woke her. God, she felt like shit. Her head was killing her, like she'd drunk an entire bottle of vodka or something, though she knew that wasn't the case.

And then that taste hit the back of her throat and she gagged, remembering what she'd ingested. It was more than just the foul flavor – she could feel the magic coursing through her veins, foreign and potent. Her skin tingled, and she swore she could see faint blue lines of energy tracing patterns beneath her skin.

"Well, at least I'm alive!" She dragged herself off the floor and headed for the door. Buttons wound around her feet – through her legs, now that she was paying attention – and meowed, though he no longer needed feeding. Which made her wonder what was eating the meat she'd been putting in the bowl out the back door. As she moved, she felt oddly light, as if gravity had loosened its hold on her. The air around her seemed to respond to her movements, swirling and eddying like an invisible cloak.

"Wow, you're looking worse for wear," June commented, before Alyssa even had a chance to process who was on her doorstep.

"I'm...not doing so great," Alyssa said carefully. She really wanted to slam the door in the woman's face, or scratch her eyeballs out, but it was as good a time as any to start sowing the seeds of revenge. A surge of power pulsed through her at the thought, and she had to consciously rein it in, afraid of doing damage. Even more afraid that the other witch might feel her power. "I don't know. It's like there's something in the house, something...malevolent. Do you...I mean, there aren't any...ghosts here or anything, are there?" She threw a glance over her shoulder and then looked back at June, hoping that the woman would mistake her unkempt appearance for fear.

Well, some of it was fear, but that had been replaced by knowledge and action, and the assistance of a handy dandy ghost. God, she needed a shower.

"Well, there were rumours, but Sylvie was a witch, so supernatural activity wouldn't have been abnormal. Is there something I can do?"

Alyssa's senses tingled, and if she were a cat, her ears would have practically twitched, picking up on the undercurrent of eagerness in June's voice. She inhaled, letting her magic expand in the space between them, watching as it seemed to shine a light on the woman's desperation. It felt complex, layered like sediment built up over decades. This wasn't just about power – it was about fear. Fear of aging, fear of irrelevance, fear of death itself.

Alyssa reached out with her hand then, not just her senses. She gripped the older woman's arm and almost jolted as flashes of June's memory popped into her mind: how June had been drawn to Sylvie's bloodline. A direct connection to Papatūānuku that her shallow magic could never achieve. She'd had spent years trying to tap into that power, first through friendship, then through love, and finally through betrayal.

It was so clear now. Alyssa felt like she'd been blind until right this moment.

June had been feeding off Gran's energy for years, stealing little bits of life force. The muffins she kept bringing weren't just baked with malice – Alyssa got the impression now that they were enchanted to weaken her defenses just as the woman had done to Gran. Using her power to steal the essence of Gran, syphon years off her life.

But Gran must have discovered the truth. Seen how June had been extending her own life by draining others, not just magically but physically. If Alyssa could see it, then surely Sylvie would have too. But maybe she really had loved June, and that love had blinded her for too long. The realisation hit Alyssa like a physical blow. June hadn't just betrayed Gran's love – she'd betrayed everything Gran had believed in. And now she was trying to do the same to Alyssa, to take not just the house and its power, but her very essence. She was a parasite, consuming others to extend her own existence, twisting the natural order of life and death. No wonder the earth itself seemed to recoil from June's presence. She wasn't just breaking rules – she was violating the fundamental principles of nature itself.

Alyssa could almost see the aura of deceit surrounding the older woman, sickly green and pulsing with malice. And she knew, now was the perfect opportunity to lay a trap. She heaved out a long, shuddering sigh, letting tears of grief and rage flow down her cheeks. "I don't know, June. I just don't know. I might head back to the city for a few days, clear my head before I decide what to do with the place."

"Oh?"

Alyssa could see that June was struggling to hide her glee at this possibility. The green aura flared brighter, and Alyssa had to blink rapidly to clear her vision.

"Yeah, it might be for the best."

"I could keep an eye on the place if you wanted me to. Water the plants, make sure no one breaks in or anything. "

Alyssa's fingers tightened around the door frame, and she swallowed bile. She felt the wood warm beneath her touch, responding to her anger. Tiny tendrils of smoke began to curl up from where her fingers met the frame, and she quickly pulled her hand away, shocked by her own power. "Yeah, that would be good. Someone should be keeping an eye on the place."

"Oh, Alyssa, I'm so sorry you're struggling with everything. A few days break to clear your head sounds like a great idea."

June laid a hand on her arm in comfort, but Alyssa slipped from her grip. The touch sent a jolt through her, like static electricity but stronger. She could feel June's magical essence trying to probe her, to gauge her power. Alyssa instinctively threw up mental barriers, surprised at how naturally it came to her.

"I need to shower. I'm feeling kind of horrible." Alyssa edged the door partway closed. "I'll call you later, before I head out of town. You'll need a key."

"Don't worry about that. I have one from your gran."

Alyssa wasn't surprised, so she just nodded. "Thanks," she said as she closed the door and threw the bolt. As the lock clicked into place, she muttered a quick protection spell under her breath, one she didn't even realise she knew. A faint blue glow emanated from the door frame before fading away.

That woman was going to pay.

"I'm having a shower. Don't watch," she called out as she headed for the bathroom. She'd have to ask where he was when he wasn't manifesting, or perhaps he was always around, but only exerted an icy chill when he wanted his presence to be known. Either way, she didn't really care right now. She just wanted to be clean and to begin acting out the lie that would ensure June fled this house permanently, and never crossed her path again.

As the hot water cascaded over her, Alyssa closed her eyes and let her mind wander. She could feel the magic within her, no longer dormant but awake and eager. It scared her, this newfound power, but it also thrilled her. Whatever Magnus had put into that drink had carved a channel directly to her magic and while it was terrifying it was also exhilarating.

She scrubbed her hair, her body, using some of the grandmother's lavender scented body wash, as if it could infuse Alyssa with some of that generational power. Give her the strength and confidence to follow through on the course she'd set.

She thought of June, of the injustices done to her grandmother, of poor Buttons. A plan began to form in her mind. She would use this power, this legacy she'd inherited, to right the wrongs done to her family. And maybe, just maybe, she'd finally find her place in this strange, magical world she'd stumbled into.

"Ready or not, June," she murmured, watching as sparks danced between her fingertips. "The new witch of Kotahi Bay is about to make her debut."

17

ALYSSA

Half an hour later, Alyssa was feeling slightly more alive, sitting on the back porch with her phone and a steaming cup of coffee. The warmth of the mug seeped into her hands, grounding her in the reality of what she was about to do. She didn't think she had it in her to take a life.

She felt the ghost before she saw him, and as she suspected, this time he didn't bring the cold with him. "So, what's the plan?" she asked. "I saw June this morning."

"I know. I was watching."

Alyssa rolled her eyes. "So, you're always watching." She glanced over at him, and he grinned.

"Always. It's not like I need to sleep." There was a

warm humour in him that she had never expected to find.

"You're surprisingly pleasant to talk to for an evil ghost that's been locked up for hundreds of years." She rested her head against the wall of the house, enjoying the warmth of the day. It would be the perfect summer if it wasn't for June and her desire for the house and the magic it possessed. Alyssa was glad that Kelly hadn't found a way to the Bay now but could imagine them out here sharing a bottle of wine, preferably without the ghost looming over them too. But he was okay. More okay than she probably deserved, considering her family track record.

"From time to time I have been set loose, but they always crossed me. Always put me back in that box." The bitterness in his voice was unmistakable, and he twitched, his form shifting out of focus for a moment. "I had all but given up hope someone would truly free me."

Alyssa felt a pang of sympathy, surprising herself. Just days ago, she'd been terrified of this entity. Now, she found herself understanding his pain, his desire for freedom. It resonated with her own journey of self-discovery.

"Well, you're lucky! There won't be any more women of our line trying to keep you captive. I have no intention of perpetuating the stupidity." She finished the last of her coffee.

"You're not actually leaving, are you?" Magnus raised an eyebrow and looked...almost concerned. As if she might slip town and forget about their deal. But it was sealed in blood now and she knew that if she tried to run, he would come after her.

There was no way she was going to bring his wrath on herself if at all possible.

"No, I'll pack my car and park it somewhere out of the way, then slip back home and help you spook the hell out of her. Have you got a plan?" Buttons approached them then, and his form seemed less solid, as though he had become more ghostlike now that she knew the truth. Still, he brushed against her side and she felt his touch, was comforted by it the same as if he'd been alive.

"She'll come as soon as you leave," Magnus predicted. "She will try to find the box, or go down into the basement to look for the necklace."

Alyssa's hand went to her chest where the necklace sat, suddenly very heavy. "This necklace?" Her voice squeaked as she asked.

"The very same," he said with a nod. "It contains my essence, and she will need it in order to control me."

Alyssa swallowed hard, her body clenching

uncomfortably under the new awareness that she was wearing his power source. Literally the thing keeping him tied to this world.

"There's a symbol on the necklace..." she said. "What does it..."

"It's a rune," he replied curtly, then his attention shifted. He gazed out into the distance as if looking into the past. "The yew tree, Eihwaz...it speaks of wisdom, of the mysteries of life and death...of passing through a gateway."

Alyssa shivered. "And what will you do?" she asked, hoping to change the topic a little.

"You will find out." His eyes glowed with what seemed to be both joy and menace, and that chill rolled off him again.

Alyssa rolled her eyes. "What am I meant to do? It's not going to be easy for me to help if you won't tell me what's going on. We're in this together, remember?"

Magnus nodded slowly. "There is a crawl space under the house. My suggestion would be for you to get under there and scrape things against the floor, make knocking noises. You know, ghostly stuff. Leave the rest to me."

Clearly, this ghost was used to being the one in control. But he knew her family was full of strong-minded women. He should know they weren't prone to just sitting around twiddling their thumbs.

"Not sure how I feel about being left out." She scrunched up her nose. "I'm not going to just let you take control of everything. Not now that I know the truth. She hurt my family. She wants to hurt me." Alyssa pressed her lips together. "I want to be there for this, so I'm going to pack the car, drive off, and then I'm coming in the back door. You don't have to tell me what you have in mind, but I'm not about to be benched in my own house."

The ghost was quiet for a moment, and then he nodded slowly, though he didn't look at her. Without another word, he vanished. She told herself that it was fine; he didn't have to trust her all the way, and it wasn't like they were going to be stuck with each other for much longer.

Part of her wished that he would let her in a little more though. Enough to know what to expect.

Alyssa glanced back out at the yard, enjoying the happy trilling of the birds in the rich, red blooms. Despite the strangeness of this past week, she loved it here and she didn't want to leave. She didn't even want to pretend to leave, though she knew she had to. It was the only way to lure June into the house.

Her eyes fell on a potted tree sitting along the left side fence. It looked like a native, though she wasn't sure what. Curiosity piqued, she moved towards it, leaving her coffee mug on the porch. An idea formed as she got closer to the tree, and when bent down she read the tag which said it was a kahikatea, or white pine.

Just what she needed.

She hefted the pot and returned to the house, her nose pressed against the narrow trunk, inhaling the earthy scent of dirt and tree. June might have ruined Gran's fake tree, but this one would be a perfect replacement. Something native, something living, something that connected her with her past and that once planted would live long into the future.

Instead of putting it in the lounge though, she placed it safely in Gran's room, lest June found a way to ruin this one too.

Feeling satisfied and hopeful, Alyssa went back to the kitchen where she grabbed some salt and random spices and headed for the basement. That sense of closeness and magic filled her even stronger than the first time she'd come down here, and she could feel a connection to the place that hadn't been there before. This was her turangawaewae, as her ancestors would have called it. Her place to stand.

Her place to take a stand as well.

She set to work on the bench with the magical supplies where she mixed and matched the items, hoping that should June try any of her witchy business, her spells would go terribly wrong. The woman deserved whatever she had coming.

As she worked, Alyssa felt a surge of confidence. This wasn't just about revenge anymore. It was about claiming her heritage, about standing up for her grandmother's legacy. She thought of Buttons, of Gran's betrayed trust, of the years of lies and manipulation. Her resolve hardened.

That task complete, she set about loading her car with several boxes from the shed and all the vintage clothing she'd found in the cupboard, and for a split second, considered actually leaving. The ghost could take care of June, but then, of course, he'd come for her – they'd made a deal. More than that, she did not want to go. She wouldn't be forced from her home now that she had claimed it.

She grinned, warmth spreading through her abdomen, the walls seeming to stand straighter, prouder, as though pleased to have been chosen.

Besides, she really wanted to be here to see what the ghost had planned.

She stuck her head into the hallway and called out, "I'm leaving now!" There was no response, but she hadn't really expected one. Alyssa pulled the door closed behind her, tears pricking her eyes all of a sudden. This felt wrong, but it was the plan. She headed for the car, quickly calling June as she went.

"Just wanted to let you know that I'm on my way," she said.

"Oh, dear. Are you okay?" June's voice was overly sweet and it grated on her.

"It's just not what I'd imagined I'd be doing so soon. I'm sure you understand. This place is special to you too."

"So special."

Alyssa could feel the undercurrent there, hear the ownership June imbued in those words.

"You'll take care of the place for me?"

"I'll treat it as if it were my own."

That was the problem. Wasn't it?

18

ALYSSA

Alyssa broke free of the bush behind Gran's house, scaled the fence with the grace of a drunk kererū pigeon, and crept to the back door. Peering inside, she couldn't see June in the kitchen, but that didn't mean a lot; she hadn't seen June come into the house any of the times she'd been playing ghost.

She toyed with the idea of returning the favor, even went so far as to find the little door at the side of the house that lead underneath before she changed her mind. Sure, she could crawl inside, figure out where June had located herself and knock on the floor. But she was embracing her witch power, right? And she had a lot more power at her fingertips now.

Too much to waste her energy pretending to be something she was not.

She'd spent almost her whole damn life doing that already.

No more.

Alyssa heard the front door click closed, and her heart raced as she realised that June was inside the house now. She both wanted to rush inside and felt frozen in place. She needed to wait though, to give June time to look for the box. Alyssa could imagine the woman's frustration when she found there was nothing but ash remaining, and no sign of the necklace anywhere.

She waited ten minutes, and it didn't sound like anything was happening in the house – she'd expected screaming by now, or something; any sign that the ghost was doing his job.

And then she did hear something, but it wasn't a scream. June was chanting, the sound low at first and then rising to fill the space, pressing against Alyssa in a magical, energetic way.

"Crap," she whispered as she ran to the back of the house. Where the hell was Magnus? And why was he not scaring the hell out of the old lady? Something had gone wrong and if she didn't get in there soon, June was going to get what she wanted.

Panic fluttered in Alyssa's chest, but beneath it, she felt a surge of determination. This was her fight too. She'd made a deal with Magnus, yes, but this was about more than that now. It was about standing up for herself, for her grandmother, for the legacy she'd inherited. It was about honoring her bargain with the ghost. Standing her ground.

Alyssa paused to kick off her shoes as she edged the kitchen door open, sending a prayer of thanks heavenward that Gran had kept all her doors oiled. Gosh, that must have pissed June off, not having any creaks to play up on when she was acting the ghost. She propped it open with one of her shoes to stop it from any telltale click.

The chanting was louder inside, not that it made any sense to Alyssa – some ancient language by the sound of it, alien to her ears despite its rhythmic tone. She grabbed the first thing that came to hand – Gran's pink floral umbrella – and snuck down the hallway towards the lounge.

When she peered around the doorframe she saw June, her eyes shut tightly, sitting in a salt circle, a ring of what Alyssa could feel were the ashes of the box that had contained the ghost inside that. Magnus was nowhere to be seen. He must have been contained by the circle. Hopefully, that was all it could contain.

Before she could contemplate the wisdom of her actions, she sprang forward and raised the umbrella, aiming for the back of June's head. The umbrella bounced out of her hand without contacting the other woman, whose eyes shot open.

"You," June hissed, her grandmotherly facade crumbling. Her eyes were vivid blue against stark white, purple veins raised on her skin. "You should have run when you could, girl. You're weak, every generation, weaker than the last. I'm trying to save us all!"

With a flick of her wrist, June conjured a swirling vortex of energy, far beyond anything Alyssa had seen Gran do. "Our power is waning. Sylvie was content to let that happen, but someone had to take action!"

In that moment, Alyssa saw the toll June's pursuit of power had taken. Deep lines etched her face, her eyes feverish with desperation. For a fleeting second, Alyssa felt a pang of sympathy. Then she steeled herself, remembering Buttons, remembering Gran.

"There are lines we don't cross, June," Alyssa said firmly. "Gran knew that. It's time you learned it too."

June's pupils expanded, wide and black, and that chant kept flowing from her mouth as if outside her will. Alyssa shivered, suddenly afraid. She wasn't just dealing with a kitchen witch here, but someone much more powerful, and far scarier than she had fathomed.

"You're an evil bitch, June. And your muffins were awful," Alyssa muttered, grinding her teeth together. She kicked out with her foot, breaking the physical aspect of the circle, but June just cackled.

"It will take more than that to breach my space, girl. You're not the witch your gran was, and even she was no match for me."

"What do you want?"

"I want the ghost. I want all his power, stored up and wasted for centuries. It's time for it to be put to use."

Alyssa turned and ran from the room as fast as she could, heading for the basement. She grabbed some of the herbs she'd tampered with and the athame, slicing it across her thumb the same way she'd done with the ghost and smearing her blood on the blade. "I don't know what I'm meant to do, but give me the strength to overcome this woman, for she means nothing but trouble." She kissed the blade and then charged up the stairs and back to the lounge. It felt as though Gran was there with her, guiding her movements, and perhaps she was.

As she ran, Alyssa felt the magic surging within her, responding to her desperate plea. She thought of her grandmother, of all the women in her line who had come before her. Their strength, their knowledge, their power – it all flowed through her veins. She was more than just Alyssa now. She was the heir to a legacy of magic, and it was time to embrace it.

Either way, she had to stop June.

June's eyes were closed again, and the air vibrated, thick with a darker kind of magic. But now Alyssa understood what she was seeing – not just malevolent power, but desperation. Decades of borrowed time catching up at last.

The necklace burned cold against Alyssa's chest as she approached the circle, athame in hand. Each step felt weighted with purpose, with generations of magic flowing through her veins. Not just her grandmother's power, but something older, something that belonged to the land itself.

"You can't win this," June said, eyes snapping open. The whites had gone completely black, like pools of oil. "You're nothing but a child playing at magic. You have no idea what true power is."

"Maybe not," Alyssa agreed, remembering Gran's lessons about hubris and balance. "But I know what it isn't. It isn't stealing life from others. It isn't betraying people who trust you."

June's laugh was hollow. "Trust? Your grand-mother trusted too easily. She never understood the sacrifices necessary for real power. Neither did any of the women in your line. Always so concerned with ethics, with balance." Her lips curled in a sneer. "That's why they kept him bound – they were too weak to use his power properly."

The room darkened as June gathered her power, shadows writhing along the walls. The temperature plunged, but this wasn't Magnus's familiar chill – this was the cold of the grave, of endings.

"Decades," June snarled. "Decades I've waited, watching your family squander what could have been mine. But you..." Her eyes fixed on the necklace. "You're the weak link. The one who ran from her power. Breaking you will be so sweet."

She thrust out her hands, green fire erupting from her fingers. Alyssa barely had time to throw up a shield – one she hadn't known she could create until that moment. The flames splashed against it, leaving trails of frost instead of burns.

Magnus's power, working through her. Protecting her.

The realisation sparked something in Alyssa's mind. June wasn't just trying to take the binding – she was trying to complete a transfer that had begun with Gran's death. If she could force Alyssa to submit, to yield her claim to the house and its magic...

"The house remembers me," June said, as if

reading her thoughts. "Remembers our magic together, Sylvie and I. Decades of spells worked under this roof. It's as much mine as yours."

But that wasn't true. Alyssa could feel it in the thrumming of power beneath her feet, in the way the very air seemed to bend towards her. The house had chosen. Just as she had chosen it.

"No," Alyssa said, power rolling through her voice. "You were a guest here. Nothing more."

She slashed the athame through the air, cutting through June's circle. Power exploded outward as the binding broke, knocking them both back.

June was on her feet just as quickly as Alyssa, and as the older woman's corrupted magic lashed out, Alyssa planted her feet firmly on the ground, feeling the strength of Papatūānuku flow up through her body. This wasn't about spells or incantations – it was about connection, about standing firm in who she was and where she belonged. "You never understood, did you?" she said to June, whose magic crackled with artificial power. "You tried to steal what can only be given. The land's power isn't something you can take – it's something you have to be worthy of receiving." The house creaked around them, and Alyssa felt the deep roots of the pōhutukawa trees stretching through the earth below, offering their strength. She wasn't just protecting her home now – she was protecting the land itself, honoring her role as kaitiaki.

The necklace pulsed against Alyssa's skin, and suddenly Magnus was there, his form more solid than she'd ever seen it.

June's eyes widened in genuine fear. "No...you can't...the binding..."

"Was never yours to control," Magnus said, his voice carrying echoes of ancient power. "You thought you could twist it to your will, use it to extend your life. But the magic knows the truth. It always has."

Alyssa found herself speaking words she didn't consciously know, her voice harmonising with Magnus's in an age-old spell of unmaking: "What was bound in blood and betrayal, let it now be undone. What was taken, let it be returned. What was twisted, let it be made right."

June screamed as the years caught up with her all at once, her stolen immortality unravelling like a frayed thread. She seemed to age decades in moments, her skin wrinkling, her hair whitening, her body becoming frail and bent.

The necklace grew colder still against Alyssa's skin. She understood now what needed to be done – not just to free Magnus, but to restore balance to the magic of this place.

"Magnus," she said softly. "It's time."

He nodded, a look of peace crossing his features. "Thank you, Alyssa Whenua. You've given me more than freedom. You've given me justice."

Alyssa reached for the necklace, feeling the last threads of the binding spell woven through it. With a quick twist, she snapped the chain. The glass beads shattered against the floor, releasing a burst of pure magical energy that filled the room with swirling lights – like the aurora, but brighter, more alive.

June crumpled, the last of her stolen years falling away. She looked ancient now, but human again. The darkness had fled her eyes, leaving only confusion and loss.

The house shuddered around them, magic realigning itself as centuries of tangled spells unravelled and reformed. Alyssa felt it settle into new patterns, centred on her – not as a prison or a binding, but as a home. A sanctuary.

Magnus's form began to fade, but he was smiling. "Remember your promise," he said. "Live well, little witch. Make this place your own."

And then he was gone, leaving only a lingering sense of rightness in his wake. The house's magic sang around Alyssa, no longer constrained by the binding spell, free to flourish as it was always meant to.

She looked down at June, huddled on the floor. The woman looked small now. All her power, her stolen years, had been stripped away, leaving only an old woman who had lost her way long ago, corrupted by the desire for more power than was rightfully hers.

Alyssa dragged the other woman out to the hallway, trying hard not to inflict any more damage, and propped her in the corner by the door before flicking her phone open and calling the emergency number. It didn't appear to connect though, so she dug through the slim paper phone book to call the local emergency services.

"Hey, um, my neighbour stopped by and she had some kind of seizure or something. She passed out in my doorway." Alyssa waited for their response and then gave the address before hanging up. June was going to be sore when she woke, but Alyssa didn't give a crap. At least it was done now, and she hadn't been the bad guy. Not entirely.

She left the older woman there and went into the lounge with the rubbish bin and broom, sweeping everything into it: athame, herbs, salt, anything she could get up. She'd just finished vacuuming the rest of the mess off the floor when there was a knock at the door.

A burly Samoan man with a neatly trimmed beard stood at the threshold. "We're here for your neighbour?"

"Yeah, sure. She's just here." Alyssa pointed to the

corner. June didn't even stir as the guy picked her up and carried her out to the ambulance. Totally weird. No stretcher or anything, just a big guy lifting an old lady. Oh well, maybe that was how they did it here in the Bay; she was going to have to get used to it. Everything was different here.

She was different here.

She closed the door behind her and leaned against it, remembering the first day she had claimed this place as her own. It felt like a lot had happened in such a short space of time, and she'd barely even had time to grieve the loss of Gran.

Or the loss of life as she knew it. She knew that grief would hit her at some point, but as she stood there, surrounded by the echoes of magic and memory, Alyssa felt a sense of peace settling over her. This house, this legacy – it was hers now. Not just by inheritance, but by choice. She'd faced her fears, embraced her power, and come out the other side stronger.

She thought of the vintage clothes waiting to be sold, of the magic thrumming beneath her skin, of the ghost who was bound to her by oath. Her life had changed irrevocably, yes. But maybe, just maybe, it had changed for the better.

She could feel a little excitement building at the beginning of a whole new adventure.

"Well, Gran," she whispered to the empty house, a smile tugging at her lips. "I guess I'm a witch after all."

And as if in response, a warm breeze swept through the house, carrying the faint scent of lavender – Gran's favorite. Alyssa closed her eyes, letting the warmth wash over her.

19

ALYSSA

It was hours later, and the light was just beginning to fade. Alyssa was bone tired, but she couldn't go to bed yet because things weren't quite over. She was hungry and distraught, and could really have done with a living cat to snuggle her. Or even Magnus, who was gone after everything with June.

June...

There was a weight in her chest when Alyssa thought of the woman and her own part in harming her. Yet, she'd been protecting her home, herself, and the ghost from someone determined to hurt them. Surely it was for the right reasons? She hated to think that the darkness in her family line had been passed down to her.

Her brain would not stop going over the events though, and she knew that despite her exhaustion there was still more work to be done.

So she sat in the lounge, on her couch, next to the potted kahikatea tree. She had found some fairy lights and threaded them through the branches, and they twinkled in near dark. It was enough festivity for now, and maybe in the next few days she'd find some new ornaments to adorn it with. Something new, something that was just hers. Perhaps a pīwakawaka to signify the death of her old life, and the birth of a new one.

Of course, there were no gifts beneath it, and she was probably going to spend Christmas alone. Strangely, that thought didn't bother her as much as it should have. Maybe that was what she needed right now – time to just be. To settle and become who she was meant to be.

Alyssa closed her eyes, letting her senses expand. She could feel the magic of the house now, a gentle thrum beneath her feet, in the walls. It felt like home in a way she'd never experienced before. Her fingers tingled with residual energy, and she marveled at how natural it felt now, this power that had once terrified her.

Alyssa felt the ghost before she saw him, the chill

of his presence wafting through the room and playing in her hair.

"I've come to say goodbye."

She swallowed hard, nerves tingling along her veins. This ghost had only been speaking to her for a few days, but they had a bond now. By blood. By shared experience.

"What happens to you now?" Alyssa turned to face him. Enough time had passed that the tinge of fear she'd felt in the circle earlier had dissipated. After all, it wasn't like he'd done anything bad to her, and he had held up his end of the deal. "I mean, you're not a genie or anything, so you can't just waft off and do whatever you like. Can you?"

"No. I'll be gone." A smile crossed his lips, the most genuine she'd ever seen on him. "Perhaps we'll meet in some other lifetime." He gave her a wink, and she couldn't help but laugh.

"Are you sure you want to go?" she asked with a shrug, trying to seem nonchalant. "You could just, you know, kick around here with me for a bit. You're not bad company."

"Neither are you, surprisingly." His eyes twinkled with mirth before dulling, a look of weary resignation replacing his amusement. "I'm ready for this to be over."

Alyssa nodded, understanding. She'd grown in

these past weeks, faced fears and challenges she never thought possible. But Magnus had been trapped for centuries. His journey was ending as hers was just beginning.

"Fair enough," she said.

"I would like to give you a parting gift, though." That smile was back, tugging at his lips.

"Yeah? Okay then. I won't say no." Alyssa's brow furrowed, not sure what to expect from this Viking ghost, but curious all the same.

Alyssa felt more awkward than ever before, and her eyes glazed with unshed tears that she refused to let fall.

“Farewell, little witch.” Magnus spread his arms wide, in a move so theatrical that he could only have picked it up from watching television. The room flooded with a cold so bitter that Alyssa shuddered and cursed Magnus for not warning her. And then she caught a glimpse of green from the corner of her eye and turned to see lights stretched out across the room. Blue and purple and yellow flickered around the edges of the green, which soared and twisted slowly across the ceiling of her lounge.

"Oh my god," Alyssa whispered, leaning back against the fireplace to watch.

An aurora in her living room. Now that was something no one else could say they'd experienced – not that anyone would believe her if she tried to claim she had. No, this was something just for her. "Thanks, Magnus," she whispered, though if this was his parting gift, he wasn't there to hear her.

She let the vision wash over her, eradicate every struggle and pain she'd felt in these last weeks, and she knew, not so deep down, actually quite close to the surface, that everything was going to be okay.

As the lights faded, Alyssa felt a sense of peace settle over her. She'd faced her fears, embraced her heritage, and come out stronger on the other side. The house no longer felt haunted or oppressive. It was hers now, truly hers, filled with potential and magic.

A knock at the door startled her from her reverie. Alyssa reached out with her senses, feeling a warm, familiar energy on the other side. She smiled, realising who it was before she even opened the door.

"Samantha," she greeted, swinging the door wide. "What brings you here?"

The blonde witch stood on the porch, a wicker basket over one arm. Her flowing skirts rustled in the evening breeze, and the scent of herbs and incense clung to her. "I felt a shift in the energy of the Bay," Samantha said, her blue eyes twinkling. "Thought I'd come check on our newest witch."

Alyssa felt a flush of pride at being acknowledged as such. She stepped back, welcoming Samantha in.

"Perfect timing. I could use some company...and maybe some advice."

They settled in the kitchen, Samantha unpacking an assortment of fresh lemon balm and other herbs from her basket. As she brewed a fragrant tea, Alyssa filled her in on everything that had happened with June and Magnus.

"You've come so far in such a short time," Samantha mused, passing Alyssa a steaming mug. The tea smelled of chamomile and something spicier – cinnamon, perhaps, or clove. "Oh, and I found something for you. Sylvie left this notebook at my house a few weeks ago. I'd been meaning to return it to her but then...well, anyway. I picked it up today and saw it was supposed to be for you."

Admiring the old-fashioned roses on the cover, Alyssa took the book, a little shiver running up her arm as she touched it. She opened it to find it was mostly empty. A purple pressed flower fell from between the pages. Beneath where it still left a ghostly imprint, she read Gran's flowing script: *For my Alyssa – when you're ready to bloom again.*

Alyssa's throat tightened. Gran had known she would find her way back to magic. Had never lost faith in her.

"She left it with you?" Alyssa asked.

Sam nodded. "I suspect she wanted us to be

friends. Sylvie was a wise woman and she must have sensed her time was running short. I can't think of any other explanation."

Alyssa shook her head slowly in wonder, tears pricking at her eyes, coming from love as much as sadness.

"How do you feel?" Samantha asked.

Alyssa took a sip, letting the warmth spread through her. She considered the question carefully. "Stronger," she said finally. "More...myself, if that makes sense. Like I've found a piece of me that was missing."

Samantha nodded, understanding in her eyes. "That's the magic, honey. It's always been a part of you. You just needed to embrace it."

They talked long into the night, Samantha answering questions and offering guidance. By the time she left, Alyssa felt more grounded, more confident in her new role.

Standing on the porch, watching Samantha disappear down the moonlit street, Alyssa took a deep breath. The air was crisp with a cold southerly wind despite the summer night, but she could smell the salt of the nearby ocean, the rich earth of the forest beyond.

She raised her hand, concentrating, and smiled as a small ball of light appeared in her palm. It danced and flickered, casting shadows across the porch. With a gentle breath, she sent it floating up into the night sky, a beacon of hope and new beginnings.

"Merry Christmas, Gran," she whispered to the stars. "I think I'm going to be okay here after all."

And as if in response, a warm breeze caressed her cheek, carrying the faint scent of lavender. Alyssa smiled. So much had changed, and now she was starting to know herself.

The next day, in the garden, Alyssa knelt beside her newly planted herbs, fingers deep in the rich soil. She felt Papatūānuku's presence all around her – in the warmth of the earth, in the surge of growth beneath her hands, in the ancient rhythm of the land itself.

Magnus was gone, released from this place where he had never truly belonged. Alyssa missed him; a soft tender feeling lingered in her chest, hoping he'd return to visit. She felt a tingle of possibility, just as she sensed that her own power would grow stronger each day as she learned to work with the land rather than trying to control it.

She understood now why Gran had chosen this specific spot in Kotahi Bay. The house sat where the energy of the earth ran strong and clear, where Papatūānuku's voice could be heard in the hum of the land.

"I'm home," she whispered, and felt the earth pulse gently in response. Not just in this house, but in this land, in this inheritance of guardianship and connection that ran deeper than blood. The ghost had taught her about breaking free from old bindings. But Papatūānuku was teaching her about forming new connections, about finding strength in belonging, about being part of something bigger.

She was Alyssa Whenua, witch of Kotahi Bay. And her story was just beginning...

EPILOGUE: BRENDAN

Brendan's footsteps echoed through the empty council building. Even in summer, these halls held a peculiar chill. The fluorescent lights flickered overhead, casting strange shadows as he made his way to Mrs Nolan's office.

She was waiting, perfectly posed behind her desk like she'd been carved there. "You're late."

"There was a problem with the boundary again." He didn't bother to apologise.

Time was running out.

"Sit,” she said.

He remained standing, pressed his hands against her desk. The wood was cool beneath his palms, grounding him. "You said you could help. That you could fix this."

"I did say that, didn't I?" She adjusted a stack of papers with precise movements. "June is...out of the way. Permanently, it seems."

Brendan sighed. "I heard as much. Perhaps this is for the best."

Mrs Nolan shook her head. "That new witch, the one in Sylvie's old place – she's stronger than June ever was. Powerful. Stay away from her."

Brendan's stomach clenched. "Sylvie's...that's two doors down from June's place?"

"Yes, I'd be careful around her." Mrs Nolan's smile was sharp as broken glass.

"I didn't come here for gossip," he said. "I need answers. My family is at risk, and you're sitting here playing politics."

"Everything is politics in Kotahi Bay, dear. Even magic." She slid a file across the desk. "But if you insist on answers...start with these. Just be careful who you trust."

As Brendan drove towards June's darkened house he noticed the other place, two doors down. Lights blazed from Sylvie's old villa.

He slowed, just for a moment.

She was there, in the window – the girl from the café. The one who'd looked at him like she could see right through him, past the tough facade to the desperation beneath. A shiver ran down his spine, though he couldn't tell if it was in recognition or warning.

As he drove away, the streetlights flickered, like the town was holding its breath, waiting to see what would happen next.

A personal message from Iris:

Hello lovelies. Thank you so much for joining Nova and I for the first book in our new series together. It's wonderful to share another magical New Zealand-based story with you, drawing on local mythology and nature.

If you enjoyed this book, please leave a rating or review to help other people find it! You can preorder In the Earths' Embrace, the next Kotahi Bay book on Kindle - we've set a nice long pre-order, with the aim to release earlier when the book is ready.

To get a sneak peak of a few characters who will be popping up in Alyssa's next novel, you can check out my book, The Witches of Holloway Road, if you haven't already, or Hexes & Vexes by Nova Blake.

If this is your first time reading my books, you might also want to check out the Myrtlewood Mysteries series, starting with Accidental Magic or the Myrtlewood Crones. If you're looking for more books set in New Zealand, you might want to take a look at my Dreamrealm Mysteries series too.

We absolutely loved writing this book and hope you enjoyed it too. Feel free to join my reader newsletter and Nova's and follow us on social media to keep up to date with our various witchy and writerly adventures.

Many blessings, Iris xx

P.S. You can also subscribe to my Patreon account for extra Myrtlewood stories and new chapters of my books before they're published, as well as real magical content like meditations and spells, and access to my Myrtlewood Discord community. Subscribing supports my writing and other creative work! For more information, see: **www.patreon.com/IrisBeaglehole**

HEXES AND VEXES CHAPTER 1

Mia stared out at the rain through the window of Lucy, her house bus. Mia firmly believed that all vehicles needed a name, and a vehicle that was also your home, even more so.

That said, she had no idea where the name Lucy had come from. The bus itself, most likely.

The rain had been coming down hard all night, leaving pools of water on the field that the travelling fair had set up camp. That always kept the customers away, and seeing as it was the last day of the fair, she figured the whole day was a washout for most of the crew. Other people were already starting to pack up their tents and displays – not many visitors came in for hula hoops and fire poi when the weather was this bad, but it didn't always deter Mia's tarot clients.

She glanced at her clock and sighed, downing the dregs of her tea and looking at the leaves in the bottom of the cup. They didn't tell her anything good. It was just going to be that kind of day. She rinsed her mug out and set it to dry on the small kitchen counter. Rufus, her foundling magpie, walked towards her and then hopped onto her shoulder, burrowing into her hair.

"I know, not the best day for a fly around the park. Sorry, bud." She ruffled his feathers, then gently removed him. He tugged on a few strands of hair in protest, then hopped away in a huff when she put him back down on the bench. "Be like that," she called after him. "I'm going to work!"

And with that, she opened the door and went down the steps into her 'office'.

It was a small bell tent – they always had the best atmosphere, and half of her job was atmosphere. One entrance led to her bus, the other to a small awning where the clients normally waited for their appointments. She lit the candles on the round card table, the warm scent of vanilla hitting her nostrils quickly, and then switched on the fairy lights and adjusted her headscarf. Finally, she picked a few tarot decks from the wooden box under her seat and scattered the table with her gems. She was ready.

Mia braced herself as she approached the door.

The tarot card reading wasn't taxing, but sometimes the people were, and she could never be sure who she'd find on the other side of the tent flap. With a final exhale, and a quick call for strength to the goddess, she opened the door.

And saw her little sister, Poppy, drenched from head to toe, water running from her black hair in rivulets.

"Poppy! What—"

The teen pushed inside the tent, and Mia noticed that Poppy was shivering badly. "What are you doing here?" Mia asked again. "Why? How?" She frowned, a million thoughts rushing through her head, and then pushed through into the bus and grabbed a blanket, before returning and draping it around the girl.

"Hi," Poppy said, and then sneezed.

All the sisterly instincts Mia thought she'd left behind rushed back in. "How long have you been out in the rain? Let me make you a hot drink or something." Mia spun back to the bus, and then stopped and turned around. "Wait. Why are you here, in the rain? Where's Camilla?"

Poppy finally looked up at Mia. Her face fell and her shoulders sagged even further, if that was possible. She must be, what, fifteen by now? A geeky looking kid that reminded Mia more of herself than she'd have liked.

"She's why I'm here," Poppy said. "Something's going on."

"Something that meant you couldn't pick up the phone and call me?" Mia raised an eyebrow. "You know I'm only a message away."

"And I know that you never come to Okato. And you need to come. Now."

Mia leaned back, surprised by the vehemence in the girl's voice. "Um—"

"No. Camilla needs you," she said. "I need you." Her voice broke, and Mia realized that Poppy was crying. She closed the distance between them and wrapped the girl in her arms. Hell, they were basically the same height now. When had that happened?

"Are you old enough to drink coffee?" Mia asked.

"I'm not a baby," Poppy said with a sniff.

"Got it. Come on." She led her little sister through the bell tent and up the steps of the bus. The girl had never been in there before; Mia had been on the road now for about six years, and they'd never managed to cross paths. AKA: their older sister refused to come and visit the travelling fair. It reeked of all the things that Camilla hated, including Mia. If they caught up it was in a café or fast food joint.

Poppy slid herself into the bench seat at the small table, while Mia put the kettle on the cooktop, then turned and leaned against the counter and eyed the teen up. The mascara on her lashes had streaked in the rain, and her freckles were barely concealed beneath a fine layer of foundation. Her thick black glasses frames gave her a librarian chic look, but underneath it all she was a girl, struggling with something.

"So, what's going on, kiddo?" Mia tried to keep her voice light. "And where is Camilla? You're not here alone, are you?"

"I hitchhiked."

Mia opened her mouth to protest, but Poppy shook her head.

"Don't say it. It's not like I've got a driver's licence. Come on, Mia."

"Fine, continue," she said with a wave of her hand. The kettle boiled and she turned away, preparing the drinks and giving Poppy the space to explain what the hell made her do such a silly thing. At her age!

To be fair, at her age, Mia had been up to all kinds of things, so she couldn't really judge.

"Cam's...changed."

"Menopause? Hormonal changes can really mess with your system. Mum went into it early," Mia said over her shoulder, pouring the milk into the mug before topping it off with boiling water and stirring.

"She's not that old." Poppy let out a big sigh. "It's hard to explain. But you need to come."

Mia slid the mugs onto the table and then frowned. "I forgot to ask if you take milk."

"It's fine. Sit."

"I'm the adult here. Aren't I meant to be giving the orders?" Mia sat anyway. "Look, if Cam has a problem, then she should be asking me for help, don't you think? It's not your job—"

"That's the thing. It is my job, because she can't... Won't... I don't know." Poppy shook her head. She wrapped her hands around the mug and sighed, her eyes closing for an instant. "It's complicated."

Mia didn't really know what to do with kids, or even teens, who were kind of like mini adults without all the wear and tear of an actual adult. But she could do this. She could.

"Okay. I'm going to need a little bit more information. Because I'd like to think you traipsed halfway across the island to find me, on your own, getting into cars with strangers, for a really good reason."

"I think..." Poppy looked into her mug, and then up into Mia's eyes. Her voice came out in a whisper. "She's different now. Cold. Erratic. I think she might have what Mum did. Or it's drugs."

Mia snorted coffee out her nose, tried to catch some of the mess in her hands, but ended up spilling the contents of her mug even further.

"What?" She dragged her headscarf off and wiped

her face with it, then dabbed at her chest, her legs, but the coffee was already soaking in. "Why would you think that?"

"Have you seen her lately?" Poppy fired the accusation back. She crossed her arms and scowled. "I came here because you're the only adult I trust. The only one that might be able to help her. To help me."

"Oh, hon." Mia reached towards her, hoping her sister would forgive the outburst, but Poppy leaned back against the seat, just out of reach. "I'm sorry. I just— Cam was always the most together girl. Organized, driven, kind." Apart from when it came to Mia, anyway. Camilla had hated Mia, for being different, for being hard, for what had happened with Chris and Georgia, and the stares from everyone in the village; which was why Poppy had come here rather than just called, Mia assumed.

She could hardly just put her on a bus and send her back to their sister if she thought Camilla was on drugs, could she? Even if that was exactly what she'd like to do.

"Yeah, well, things have changed. Big time. And I need her, so you need to come home because I'm just some dumb kid who's figured it out, so it must be really bad."

Poppy glared at Mia, and for a second she saw the echo of Camilla's rage at her. But this was the sister who loved her, who thought she was cool. Who thought her life, travelling around the country, doing readings for clients, was badass.

Right? Or had she blown it with this one too?

"Okay." Mia nodded as she stood up. "I'll come, but you owe me for this, kiddo. You know I can't stand that place, so you have to have my back. Got it?" She dumped her coffee in the sink and rinsed out the mug, putting it next to her tea cup from earlier. "Now, I have clients, and you need to get out of those wet clothes. If you're smart enough to find your way to me, you're smart enough to find some dry ones."

And with that, Mia swept from the bus, back to her bell tent and her first actual customer of the day. Any problem they threw at her had to be better than wondering if her big sister was a drug addict, or heading into early onset dementia like their mother.

WITCHES OF HOLLOWAY RD PROLOGUE AND CHAPTER 1

The light of the waxing harvest moon slipped silkily over the ivy that clung to the weatherboard of the cottage near the end of Holloway Road.

Light flickered through the windows.

Inside, Sorrel and Esme Cauldwell braced themselves as they leaned over the small cauldron, their white hair tied back in scarves, and their wrinkles deepened by the low light of candles.

Esme threw a bundle of mugwort, sage and thyme, into the cauldron. The smoke rose in plumes, forming intricate patterns, as the herbs burned aromatic against the hot charcoal. Esme squinted into the smoke, allowing her mind to relax and let the patterns reveal themselves. "It's time, Sorrel," she said to her sister.

"I know the energy has been building for a while, but she's still young," Sorrel said. "She's not going to listen to a couple of old biddies like us."

"It's her Saturn Return," said Esme. "She needs to come back here for her powers to set in."

"That was the exact thing that sent her mother packing, remember," Sorrel replied. "That girl hasn't been back here in twenty years, despite all our visits. What makes you think she'll come back now?"

"She'll come back," Esme said, assuredly. "Because we're going to need her to housesit for us."

"We are?"

Esme raised her eyebrow, cunningly. "Oh yes, and you know, she's a sweet thing with nowhere else to go right now, how could she refuse a request like this from her dear old grandmother?"

"Where are you expecting us to go, then?" Sorrel asked.

"It's time for another trip to Bermuda, don't you think?" Esme strode over to the oak armoire and pulled out a tattered scroll of paper. "My list of questions for the Arch Magistrate is getting rather long, after all."

Sorrel laughed. "Of course you do! And what will

you tell Ursula? That we've gone to lobby the witching parliament?"

Esme narrowed her eyes at her sister. "Of course not. It will be a while until she's ready for all that, but it will come in time. You know she has to connect with the witching world, it's in her destiny. Even old Galdie Thorn foretold it, may her spirit rest in peace."

Sorrel chortled. "You know as well as I that Galdie will be as busy in the spirit world as she was in this realm, not to mention keeping an eye on her descendants. I hear the Thorn girls are getting themselves into quite some trouble over in Myrtlewood and I'm sure they're just getting started."

Esme couldn't help but smile at that and then turned her attention back to the scrying smoke. "Oh, Sorrel! Look what you've done to the magic – you've sent it all over the place with your mischievous mind – as usual!"

Sorrel grinned and watched the smoke for a moment. "All that passes is surely meant to be."

Esme let out a grumble. "You always say that, and yet you know we believe in the power of will, especially where a witch is concerned."

"Destiny, will and chaos!" Sorrel crowed. "The three strands woven by the fates themselves. And from what the herbs are telling me, Ursula's destiny may well be entwined with Myrtlewood too – if she can ever connect with her magic."

"It's settled then," said Esme. "I'll call her tomorrow."

Sorrel tutted. "Always so hard-headed. Are you sure we can't stick around to help her figure things out?"

Esme shook her head. "You know as well as I do that she has to do this on her own. We can cast extra protections on the cottage to keep her safe." Esme's expression hardened.

"Oh..." said Sorrel, suddenly solemn. "Oh, I see. Ursula's powers coming in will open up more than just her own magic. It will—"

"It can't be helped," said Esme.

"But she doesn't know anything. She'll be completely vulnerable. No. We mustn't."

Esme smiled sadly. "It's the only way, Sister. Ursula will have to come into her powers, one way or another, and Holloway Road is the best place. She'll simply have to face whatever may come with it."

Chapter 1

Ursula Cauldwell stepped off the bus and into the Wellington wind. She pushed her dark hair out of her face and shivered, partly from the cold and partly from an un-named thrill that ran through her.

I'm finally back in the Aro Valley...after so many years.

Ursula buttoned her red woollen coat. Auckland had been much warmer, though she hadn't noticed the temperature when she'd caught the bus from the airport.

Exhausted and still burdened from the life she's left behind, she dragged her luggage down a more gentrified Aro Street than the one she vaguely remembered. Most of the old villas and cottages had clearly been painted and refurbished, with newer houses cropping up in between them in faux old-fashioned styles.

Though there was still daylight in the last minutes of the late afternoon, the streetlights had already turned on.

As she neared the corner that took her closer to Holloway Road, Ursula felt a renewed energy. Some of the weariness she'd been carrying with her from the breakup and the betrayal and the anguish of the past few weeks melted away as new a sensation shimmered through her torso and down her limbs.

The streetlight above her flickered.

At first, Ursula thought nothing of it, but by and by she recalled walking down the same street twenty years before with her grandmother, Esme, who had stared up the flickering light and said, "Oh, bother."

"What is it?" the child Ursula had asked.

"Another surge," Gran replied.

"Surge of what?"

"Oh, don't you worry. It's nothing for us to be afraid of. Just the energy doing its thing."

The now-grown Ursula shook her head and walked on, trying to dislodge the memory. It had surfaced, raw in a way she couldn't quite explain.

Leaving this place as a child had felt wrong, even though she'd had no choice. After they'd left—well, Violet made sure they never returned to visit. Something precious had been torn from her; now all the memories carried that ache with them.

She continued walking, right to the beginning of Holloway Road. The streetlight above her flickered as well.

...Must be something up with the grid.

~

THERE WAS a certain sense of stillness at the entrance to Holloway Road, where the quirky suburbia of Aro Street gave way to hints of native forest at the periphery of the reserve, as if the land was taking a breath. A stranger to this place might think there was no more to see, but Ursula knew there was always a new level of depth within this part of the world, feeling it as she took her next steps into Holloway Road—a valley within a valley, almost an island of its own.

Ursula looked up at the familiar sight of the forested hill to her right, and then towards the small park to her left. She, too, took a breath, before being flooded with memories: bright red boots, the yellow bucket she'd carried everywhere she went as a child, gathering herbs and stones to make charms and spells as she played her favourite games.

She stopped in the middle of the path to inhale the scent of moss and lichen, mulched leaves and cut grass, reminding her she was finally coming home. Auckland had never felt like this. It irked Ursula that she'd been kept away from this place for so long, despite never belonging anywhere else.

Here there were few houses under a hundred years old, and though some of them now looked much nicer than the dreary run-down shacks she remembered from her childhood, the history of the place hung, syrupy, in the air.

A dark jewelled gleam caught her eye in the low light.

Blackberries. Perfectly plump and just waiting to be foraged. She couldn't help but reach out and pluck them, mindful of avoiding the thorns. Their juice stained her hands like blood, and taste exploded in her mouth, complex and tangy. It sent an unexpected shiver through her body. Tingles ran down her arms and spine in a way that reminded Ursula of the old saying...*someone's walking on my grave...*

A streetlight flickered again. Ursula glanced back towards it to see a glimpse of someone. A stocky man in a white suit, his oily dark hair slicked back.

She blinked and he was gone. Ursula felt a chill that was nothing to do with the cold wind.

Surely I just imagined that...I must be tired.

It wasn't that she didn't believe in apparitions or spirits or psychic phenomena, *per se*; they just never happened for her.

There were certainly ghosts here, with so much history.

Ursula vaguely recalled old stories of a murder, of police raids, activism, and even a mysterious disappearance: a young woman who went missing long ago, never to be seen again.

The place was almost a living thing, all knitted together into a rich tapestry of wilderness and potlucks, intrinsically connected to the real power holding the whole place together.

But that man didn't belong here. No, he was more the stuff of nightmares—of her imagination running wild on a dark night—than of anything truly mystical, she decided.

It was just before dusk, and the starlings were congregating as they always did, murmuring themselves into a fervour. In Ursula's imagination they asked each other, *is it time yet? Is it time?* And then the oldest, wisest one, with a streak of grey at her temples called, *NOW!*

They all took flight.

ACKNOWLEDGMENTS

A big thank you to all my wonderful Patreon supporters, especially:

John Stephenson
Danielle Kinghorn
Ricky Manthey
Wingedjewels
Elizabeth
Rachel
and William Winnichuk

ABOUT IRIS BEAGLEHOLE

Iris Beaglehole is many peculiar things, a writer, researcher, analyst, druid, witch, parent, and would-be astrologer. She loves tea, cats, herbs, and writing quirky characters.

facebook.com/IrisBeaglehole

x.com/IrisBeaglehole

instagram.com/irisbeaglehole

ABOUT NOVA BLAKE

Nova Blake is a Māori/Pākehā speculative fiction author from Aotearoa New Zealand. She enjoys coffee (and lots of it), devouring good stories (in any format), and sleep (though she never gets enough).

Printed in Great Britain
by Amazon

61634309R00139